Serving Serena

Candice Butler

Copyright 2015

Fifty-something artist, Serena Davies desperately needs inspiration. At an artists' retreat she finds it in the form of the gorgeous, sexy, thirty-something hard body named Anteros, assigned to assist her. Anteros plans to fulfill Serena's every desire.

Serena knows an older woman with a younger man is asking for trouble. Still she can't resist Anteros pull. He's not just any gorgeous Greek, he's the Greek god of requited love, and he's determined to serve Serena.

SERVING SERENA – Oh My Gods Series – Book 1
ISBN
ALL RIGHTS RESERVED
Copyright 2015 Candice Butler
Cover Art by Jimmy Gibbs
Edited by Bonnie Walker

Dedication
Thank you to the three who have been with this project from day one, husband James and friends Karen and Judith. Also, thank you to all the women of a certain age who have taught me so much, most important of which is, "we're never too old for passion."

Chapter One

I could barely make out the fog shrouded contours of the small private island in the distance as the ancient tug wheezed over the crest of another wave. Clinging to the rail, I swallowed hard, willing the light lunch I'd eaten to stay down. Finally a long wooden pier came into view. The engines throttled back and the boat sidled toward it, fighting against the strong wind.

A brown hooded figure stood at the end of the pier. He reached out, gripped the thick rope and wrapped it over the rail. The tug engines dropped to an idle.

The deck hand passed my bags to the waiting figure.

"Good luck Miss," he said helping me from the heaving deck onto the bottom rung of a ladder attached to the dock.

"Thanks," I said. Salt water splashed into my face, cutting off anything else I might have wanted to say, like "Wait, don't leave me here!" Had I really called the St. Catherine of Bologna Monastery to beg for a residency? What was I thinking? Simple, I was burned out and desperate. For two months I'd bummed around my Queen Anne Hill studio, unable to create so much as a crayon drawing, let alone enough works for a major showing.

The tug boat slammed against the bottom of the ladder and for an instant my feet dangled in mid-air. Before the scream left my throat, a strong hand reached down, grabbed my wrist and hauled me up the final rungs. Electricity pulsed through me from that grip. And if I hadn't been terrified, it would've been a turn on.

"Thank you."

Most of his face remained obscured by the hood, only peridot green eyes met mine.

"You're welcome," the monk said.

Despite the howling wind, his voice sounded soft and sexy, almost as if he'd spoken directly into my thoughts.

"This way." He flung the two heavy duffle bags containing my easel, paints, stretchers, canvas, and brushes over his shoulders as if they weighed nothing. Then he picked up the battered suitcase holding my clothes, and headed off the dock toward a flagstone path. I followed head down against the wind.

"Ahhh!" A gust of wind ripped the rain hat from my head, sending it skittering along the ground. The monk dropped my bags. Rushing forward, he chased the hat, finally capturing it beneath the toe of his sandaled foot. The robe swirled round his body, revealing what looked to be a pair of really great legs, the kind that utility kilts, the heavy canvas, multi-pocketed version of the Scottish garment, were made for.

I watched him bending over until a errant gust knocked me back a step and whipped salt sodden hair across my eyes. I brushed it away in time to see the question I'd pondered since first laying eyes on him in that brown robe, answered.

Boxers or briefs?

He'd chosen neither. A small gasp escaped me as I caught a glimpse of one muscular butt cheek and a quick side view of the thick base of his cock and substantial balls. An even stronger flash of lust went through me.

He walked back holding my hat. I looked down at it, afraid my thoughts were clearly written on my face.

Stop it Serena, he's a man of the cloth! I chided myself. My current situation could be blamed in part because I'd lusted after the wrong man.

Work, that's all I had time or energy for if I wanted to save my career.

Our hands touched as he passed me my hat. Electricity again, I must be imagining it. He scooped up my bags and continued up the pathway.

The path ended at a doorway to large log cabin.

"Meals and gatherings happen in the great room." He opened the door so I could look in at a large, inviting room. Colorful woven tapestries hung against the smooth log walls, from tall vaulted ceilings to floor, and a huge rock fireplace took up the entire wall at one end. In front stood a long table lined by chairs. The other end of the room had been divided into cozy areas of comfortable looking chairs and sofas. A black iron stove burned cheerily in the corner.

I relaxed a little. Okay, all of this looked pretty normal, even comforting. I'd heard the retreat made remarkable changes in artists. An artist I knew described her experience as like having her soul ripped away and replaced with something more profound.

After two months of staring at blank canvases, almost paralyzed by the thought of picking up a brush or pencil again, I was ready to try anything. I had to paint or perish.

I'd been waiting my entire career for a chance like an exclusive showing at the Reynolds Gallery. If I did well there, I'd never have to worry about hustling my paintings myself again. At least that's what Michael Reynolds told me when I'd signed the contract to show.

"Your studio is this way." The monk said pulling me from this memory. As we walked around the side of the building my breath caught in my throat. The monastery buildings sat in a cathedral of towering cedars. Striated tree trunks reached so high I had to crank my neck backward to see where the deep green branches started. Gold, orange, yellow, and pink dahlia beds lined the walkway. Beyond, bright green vegetable plants huddled atop tidy mounds of dark earth.

Nestled among the grove of trees discreet distances apart were cottages, each one painted to blend with its startling beautiful surroundings. The pungent odor of evergreens and salt air filled my head, while the sound of the surf crashing against the rocks soothed my mind.

"This is beautiful," I said.

"Yes, very much so." He adjusted the bags over his shoulder as his gaze rested on me. "There's a path down to the beach, over there." He pointed to an opening between two enormous cedars.

We followed a well-worn foot path. The monk stopped in front of a cottage with a dark green door.

"You're in Pinewood," he said.

He opened the door, stepping aside for me to enter first. I sucked in another breath. Through the large window across the room, slate-colored waves met a pewter sky. Tree tops poked upward from further down the cliff. In the distance whitecaps danced across the surface of Puget Sound.

"This is breathtaking." I rushed over to the window and stood, taking in the magnificent view. If I couldn't get inspired to paint these landscapes, I might as well hang up my brushes for good.

Behind me I heard him open the small stove and deposit some wood inside.

"Things should warm up fairly quickly." The stove door squealed with protest as he closed the latch.

When I turned around he stood behind me, so close I felt the heat penetrating through his robe, reminding me of that glorious cock I'd caught a glimpse of earlier. Was it long as well as thick? My heart slammed against my ribcage. Neither of us moved.

"Did you want your bags left by the window?" he asked, finally speaking.

"Uh, what?"

He smiled. The robe now covered his eyes, but his mouth was beautiful too. I found myself wishing I could see the whole package at once, rather than only catching a tantalizing piece of him at a time. He bobbed his head in the direction of my duffel bags.

"Yes – yes, please leave them here by the window. I'll unpack them later. "

His hand shot out from the voluminous robe sleeve, grasping the bags with strong fingers. I studied the big hands, with veins tracing pathways to worn knuckles, and long fingers. The nails were rounded and cut short. Each fingertip had a covering of rough callus, like he'd spent a lot of time running those fingers over textures. The muscles in his forearm roped, and then relaxed as he set the bags down. He obviously did work that required the use of muscles and sinew.

What would those callused finger tips feel like squeezing my nipples or sliding over my clit? That strong right hand slipped back into the belled sleeve of the robe.

This had to stop. I hadn't seen the inside a church in over three decades, but I still had enough Catholic in me to know seducing a monk would land me straight in hell. This sudden horniness had already turned me into a complete idiot. Eternal damnation was not an option I wanted to contemplate.

Taking a deep breath, I slammed a lid down on the hormonal fire. Was this new appreciation of everything male just another pang of menopause, like the hot flashes and those temporary memory lapses?

"Anything else Ms. Davies?" he asked.

"No thank you. Please call me Serena."

"Teros." He moved to leave.

"Will I see you again Teros?" *Good one. It's an island, of course you're going to see him again.*

"I'm assigned to you. So I'd say that's a certainty, Serena."

"I don't need anyone … What do you mean assigned to me?"

"You came here to work, to create. " He smiled again, warming me in spite of my soaking clothes and hair. "To support the addition of beauty to the world through art is the reason for this monastery. Therefore the order assigns someone to serve each artist in residence, so the artist can use all of their time to explore themselves, their art and to create."

He paused, gifting me with that smile again.

"I'm here to serve you, Serena."

My artist friend hadn't mentioned that part.

"Uh, thank you."

"Would you like some help unpacking now?"

"No thank you, I'll get it later. Right now I'd like to soak up this wonderful place."

"Of course. Dinner is in an hour, unless you'd like me to bring you a tray."

"No, I'm anxious to meet the others."

"Good. I'll see you there." Teros slipped out quietly.

Pulling out a sketch pad and pencil I sketched the stunning view outside the window. He had such arresting eyes. I ripped the landscape drawing from the pad and set it aside. I'd not get any work done until I got those eyes out of my head.

Eyes are the hardest things to draw well for me. Yet his I had no problem with. My pencil moved on its own, sketching almond shaped eyes with long curling lashes, sensuous heavy lids that hid pain and humor. I needed to capture that sparkling yellow-green that reminded me of the richest peridot or a large feral cat. I rifled through one my bags until I located the box of pastels and went to work shading in the colors.

Somewhere outside, the deep round tone of a gong being struck pulled me away from my drawing. I looked down at my renderings with satisfaction. They weren't landscapes, but they did have the emotional resonance my work had been missing lately. I'd done three separate pieces in little more than an hour, Teros' eyes, his arm and hand, the lifted folds of his robe with his strong legs and glimpse of his butt, scrotum, and a hint of penis.

I hadn't been able to paint or draw for months, yet these sketches poured out of me without effort. It wasn't quite having my soul ripped away, but something about this place was definitely working for me.

Chapter Two

The smell of fresh baked bread and grilled beef filled the great room. All of the chairs at the table were occupied with the exception of one. Not wanting to keep everyone waiting, I hurried over to sit down. Besides, after weeks of brooding, living off coffee and whatever required no preparation, my mouth watered at the thought of a real cooked meal.

A gorgeous African-American woman in a green sweater and a Mariner's baseball cap plucked some papers from the seat.

"Sorry, I forgot you were coming today. I'm Danielle Michaels, poet."

"Serena Davies, painter."

"Cool. " She waved the papers in her hand. "I'm reading right after dinner. It's a work in progress. I'd love to have your feedback."

"Sure. But I really don't know much about poetry," I said.

"Everybody says that, but they know what makes them feel and think. "

I noticed the woman across the table nudged Danielle's foot with hers. Their eyes met and I'd have had to be blind to not see the flash of desire that passed between them.

"I'm May Nguyen, "an exotically beautiful Asian woman said.

Black eyes held mine for a moment while she sized me up. Her skin glowed pale and flawless in the low light.

"I also write."

I reached out my hand to clasp hers briefly.

"Nice to meet you."

"I think I've seen some of your work," May said. "Don't you have a book out with a series of mountain landscapes?"

"Yes. It was published a couple of years ago."

"Your paintings are fantastic. You know, I never thought of landscapes being erotic, but yours, with all those rugged, phallic peaks standing over yearning, wide thighs, oops, I meant valleys, definitely changed my mind."

"Thanks, I think."

May's laughter tinkled softly. "Remembering them gets me all hot and bothered." She looked soulfully at Danielle, whose dark brown eyes widened in response.

"May writes erotic literature," Danielle explained. "She's really huge in England."

Three monks walked in from the kitchen carrying large wooden salad bowls. I must have gasped aloud, because I heard Danielle laugh softly.

"Yes, Teros is quite exquisite," she whispered.

Finally I could view his whole face at once. The hood of his robe draped over his shoulders. He was beautiful and I truly couldn't think of another word to describe him. Longish black hair swept carelessly to one side, brushing against dark olive skin and the light stubble of an evening shadow. He appeared to be mid-thirties, probably only a few of years older than my son.

Teros eyes met mine, sending a jolt through me. Stopping behind May, he placed the salad bowl in the center of the table.

"Tonight George has prepared salad Nicoise, mushroom risotto, beef medallions with Madeira truffle sauce and strawberry tarts. He apologizes the meal is not up to his usual standard." Teros announced.

Then he and the other two served the salad into bowls. When he finished he left without another word.

"What's that about?" I asked.

"George makes them make that announcement every night. He's some hoity toity chef with restaurants all over the world. I've yet to figure out what his usual standard is, because everything he's sent out of that kitchen since I've been here is food fit for the gods," Danielle said.

"Here, here," an intense looking man in black rimmed glasses said. "I'm Richard Ware, composer."

I smiled at him. "Serena Davies."

"Rumor is he suffered some kind of nervous breakdown or crisis of confidence and came to Saint Cats to recover," Richard said.

Teros returned with a bottle of wine. He paused at each place, asking before filling the glass with a dark red vintage.

"This is excellent Beaujolais, would you care for some Serena?" he asked quietly over my shoulder.

I squirmed, trying to ignore the flood of heat settling in my pussy and suddenly remembered my embarrassing crush on Father Gerard, at sixteen. I'd confessed to him that I thought about having sex with boys, just to see what he'd say. Father Gerard said thinking about boys is normal, but I should say twenty Hail Mary's whenever I felt temptation. Good advice, I would probably up the number to 50 or so to be on the safe side before I retired tonight.

"Yes, thank you."

His arm brushed against my breast as he reached over my shoulder to fill the glass. My nipples snapped to attention, pressing against the light sweater I wore. Across the table, May gave me a knowing look, licking her cherry red lips.

I'm here to paint, not blaspheme.

Afraid to catch Teros' eye again, I concentrated on the plate put in front of me and tried to focus on the various conversations around me.

Danielle had been right. George's "not-up-to-usual- standards-meal" was extraordinary. The expertly prepared food seemed to call to some emotional need beyond mere hunger. I groaned, eventually pushing away the last tender bites of beef.

Teros swept up the plate and placed a miniature masterpiece of bright red strawberries surrounded by flaky crust in front of me.

"I can't eat another bite."

"I'll put it in the refrigerator in your room, for when you get hungry later." He picked up the tart. I didn't have the heart to tell him I never got hungry after dinner.

More conversation and the wine bottles got passed around until empty. By this time my eyes felt like they'd been filled with sand, while the rest of me sagged from tired bones.

Finally everyone pushed back from the dinner table. A couple of people left but most wandered over to the seating area at the opposite end of the room to chat and share their work.

I touched Danielle's arm as she headed in that direction.

"I'm really sorry and I'd love to hear your poem, but I'm worn out."

"Don't worry about it. I've been working on this piece for a while. You'll get plenty of opportunities to hear it." Her expression turned sympathetic.

"Between that buckboard boat trip over and the whole anxiety thing of coming to a place like this, everybody's first night is pretty much a wash."

"Yeah," May chimed in. "We were actually surprised you made it to dinner. Most of us spent that first night in our cottages."

"Okay, then I'll see you tomorrow."

"Tomorrow." they said in unison and then walked over, arms entwined, to join the others.

I followed the well-lit path back to my cottage. As I pushed open the green door I knew immediately someone had been here. My suitcase no longer sat in the middle of the floor. I could also see my clothes hanging in the closet.

The easel had been assembled and a blank five-foot canvas tacked to stretcher bars sat on it next to the window. Where had that come from? I hadn't brought anything that size with me, because I'd hoped a smaller series would be faster to paint.

Paints, pallet, and brushes, charcoal, pencils and pastels were neatly arranged on the table next to it. I walked over, and ran my fingers each tool. They'd been laid out exactly the way I would've done it.

I saw the just-in-case box of condoms, supersized vibrator, and lubrication tucked into the partially open drawer of the nightstand. Okay, a little embarrassing.

From the doorway to bathroom I caught the flicker of candlelight. Tiny candles burned on the stand next to the old fashioned claw-footed tub. The smell of lavender and vanilla floated through the humid room.

Teros! Oh-mi-god, I'd left my drawings of him lying on the bed. I hurried out of the bathroom. The hand pieced quilt had been turned back, the pillows fluffed and my drawings stacked neatly on the table in front of the couch. A note written in bold masculine scrawl lay atop them.

Your talent is astounding, I'm flattered. Should you require a model, I am here to serve you. Sleep well Serena. Teros.

Okay, even more embarrassing.

Could Teros actually be flattered that some old broad rendered his genitals in pastels? I picked the drawings up, spreading them out again. They were good, some the best work I'd done in a long, long, while, maybe ever.

I restacked the drawings and tucked them into the back of my portfolio. Perhaps my spark had returned and if so it seemed all due to Teros. Every time he'd leaned over my shoulder to set down or pick up a dish, I'd thought about him being naked beneath that robe. My hands itched to rip it off him.

Hopefully, he'd missed the sexual hunger that had poured out of me onto those pages and think I'd simply taken a lot of artistic license.

I got undressed, assessing myself in the mirror. Sophia had referred to me as an earth mother and she hadn't meant it as a compliment. I still had pretty good breasts, not too saggy, yet. So maybe I had a little more than the HWP referred to in the personals. I'm an artist. I let my work do the talking for me. After undressing, I eased down into the scented water, finding it the perfect temperature.

My fingers moved to my clit that pulsed beneath a mound of bubbles. The ends of his fingers had been tipped with tiny calluses. What had he done to get those calluses and how would those rough tips feel sliding over my clit or buried deep inside me? Is it a sin to think about a monk while masturbating? Did monks secretly masturbate?

I doubted if May and Danielle had to go the do-it-yourself route. They're fabulous bodies were almost exact opposites, and probably fully engaged with each other at this moment.

Danielle was petite and curvaceous to the point of being Rubenesque. Her full rounded breasts perched atop her tiny waist.

May on the other hand was tall, straight and willowy, with lovely long legs and barely perceptible breasts beneath her tee shirt. The two women's inability to keep their hands off each other during dinner made it pretty obvious what they would be doing afterwards.

Oh well, something good could be said for solitude. And if I sat here long enough playing with myself, I might be able to figure out what.

Slipping two fingers inside my heat, I moved them in and out, relishing the tingle that coursed through me. Easing deeper into the soothing water, I remembered his intense green eyes, the strong hands that had hefted my bags, yet wrapped the delicate stem of the wineglass. My breath caught as I brought to mind his thick penis and those beautiful heavy sacks swinging beneath it. I longed to see the whole thing and feel it inside of me. And I never would.

If daydreaming about Teros' exquisite body and about fucking him, right now, would lead me to a fiery eternity later, frankly, I didn't give a Hail Mary.

"Damn it! Why can't I get this to work?"

May slammed her hand against the keyboard on her laptop sending the cursor into a fit of x's and z's.

Danielle came up behind her and leaning over, and slid her lips down the slender column of May's throat.

"You're brilliant, so don't worry. It will come," Danielle whispered.

Letting her caress follow the path of her kisses, Danielle slipped her hand under the front of May's shirt. May shivered; her dark hair cascading down as she tilted her head back. Danielle's lips captured those of her lover.

"Hmm, you're not wearing a bra." She lifted up the tee shirt, squeezing the russet gold of May's half dollar sized nipples.

May groaned, leaning into the pressure of Danielle's kneading fingers.

"Maybe to write about a good fuck, I need to have one first."

She stood up, and tugged Danielle's sweater over her head.

"Her hungry eyes gazed at the deep line of cleavage and the soft dark caramel globes barely contained by her lover's scrap of black lace brassier," May said roughly.

"Good line, should I be taking notes?" Danielle asked.

Undoing the front clasp of Danielle's bra, May let the large breasts bounce free.

"They seemed to scream to be touched, kissed, suckled." May's hands slid underneath lifting the breasts up. She raised one high, teasing Danielle's lips with her own nipple. Danielle's eyes shut as she pulled the nipple between her lips.

"Hmm, that's it baby. I love to watch you do that." May murmured before taking Danielle's other breast into her mouth. Danielle stopped her own ministrations to watch May lavish her breast with tongue and teeth. She moaned each time May gave her a gentle bite.

"I need to touch you," Danielle said.

Tongues shot out as their lips met and their hands grappled at each other's pants. Danielle won, letting May's jeans drop and sliding her fingers between pale skin and bright red panties.

May's knees sagged.

"Stop, I need you on the bed," she said on a ragged breath.

Their mouths clasped briefly, and then they hurriedly stripped off the rest of their clothes. While each had been beautiful separately, wrapped in each other's arms they were glorious together. Creamy brown skin contrasted against milky pale, tiny breasts pressed against, full breasts, Danielle's womanly hips cradling May's more angular ones.

"I hope this helps you write that next chapter," Danielle said, stretching May out on the bed.

May's long limbs trembled as Danielle slid her hand over them.

Gently she spread those the long tapering legs and slid her head between them. May moaned, arching upward. Danielle ran her finger down the inside of May's thighs and then kissed her way up them. May fisted the quilt with both hands. Danielle kissed the silky dark hair of her lover's pussy, before her tongue shot out to take a delicate lick at her clit. May reached out taking Danielle's head between her hands.

"Stop teasing!"

"Patience. Think of this like your books, the longer you make them wait for it, the better it is."

She slid two fingers into Mays' slick folds.

"Um, that's it, relax, and let me work."

Danielle kissed the pussy lips and slipped her tongue inside. May cried out.

"Swing around, I need to taste you too,"

May rolled onto her side, bending until her mouth reached Danielle's pussy.

"Hmm, you smell sweet," she nuzzled

"This may not help you with the words, but I can help you find the emotions," Danielle said.

"Did I mention that I love you?" May asked.

"Hmm, I love you too."

Chapter Three

I awoke with a start, splashing now cold bath water over the candles which sputtered and went out. What a dream! How long had I been asleep?

Jumping from the tub, I grabbed the thick terry robe from the back of the door, and wrapped it over my shivering body. No time to dry off, I needed to get this down. The easel sat waiting for me with the large canvas, sized, ready and perfect for what I needed to paint.

Thank you Teros.

My pencil seemed to glide across the surface on its own as I tried to get the outlines down before they left my head.

Danielle's sensuous thick lips, the curve of her neck and the heavy succulent fullness of her naked breast, nipples oversized Hershey's kisses, brown and sweet, the womanly "S" of her small waist, the rounded swell of her stomach and wide hips, like rolling hills that plunged into the deep rich valley between her thighs, poured out of the pencil first.

Eyes are always the hardest. I often thought not being able to imbue eyes with a lifelike quality and genuine emotion were the reasons I'd shied away from painting people, sticking to landscapes, fruit and flowers instead.

Danielle's eyes were large warm toffee-colored pools, full of intelligence and mischief. When they rested on May they'd turned smoky with desire and soft with love.

I used the charcoal, filling in the dark pupil; too much. I grabbed the eraser, removing the darkness, then smudged it with my thumb. Still not quite right. Dabbing, smudging, erasing, cursing, I don't know how much time passed. I put down the charcoal finally satisfied. Danielle stared up at me from the canvas, those eyes challenging and a dimpled smile turning up the corners of her mouth.

God, I was starving. I dug my cell phone out of my purse to check the time. The kitchen probably wouldn't be open at three in the morning. I continued the search through my purse hoping for a Luna bar I hadn't already found and eaten. I located a cough drop and a package of crushed crackers from the last meal I'd eaten before climbing onto that boat, a cup of chili and a side salad.

Ripping through the cellophane, I emptied the cracker crumbs down my throat, only to start a coughing fit. A pitcher of water along with a glass sat on the table next to the bed. I said another silent thank you to Teros as I gulped it down. Note to self: the downside of coming to an island - no all-night restaurants.

Salvation! I remembered the lovely strawberry tart Teros said he'd to put in the refrigerator.

On the second shelf sat the tart wrapped in plastic, above to it a sandwich on whole wheat bread with the crusts removed, a carton of milk, and a card that read:

I hope you like turkey. Teros

How? I loved turkey. Did everyone get this kind of service? I would ask him tomorrow. I finished off the first sandwich half in two bites. It was perfect, almost as if he'd known I loved the dark meat and dill relish as the only condiment.

After wolfing down the second half and the tart and finishing off the milk, I returned to my sketching.

May's exotic beauty proved harder to capture. Unlike Danielle's relaxed, front forward, lying on her side pose, May slid onto the canvas at an angle. One long willowy arm slid between Danielle's soft thighs, while the other hand reached for the pendulous breast, thin fingers settling across the flesh as light as a butterfly resting on a leaf.

Draped across Danielle's lower half, May's body appeared strung tight, ready, like a fine bow waiting for the release. One pale butt cheek clenched in anticipation. I smudged at the shadow of the hollowed muscle, removing some of the charcoal to bring up the reflected light.

Her oval face tilted to one side and her nimble tongue licked pouty red lips with promise and preparation. Silky black hair concealed one eye. Okay, doing only one eye might be cheating, but the other looked at Danielle with a mixture of love and playfulness.

Holding onto inspiration often felt like trying to hold water in your hands. It could slip away so easily. I looked at the outline on the canvas knowing tonight I'd managed to hold onto at least part of it.

I twisted off the tops of paint tubes and began squirting them onto the palette, going fast and mixing colors on the fly, half afraid I would forget those perfect colors of hair, skin and eyes, the bright yellow of the curtains, the rich greens and blues of the quilt they made love on.

Taking a deep breath, I dipped into the golden-red, sepia I'd mixed, dabbing it onto Danielle's leg. It glowed with the warmth and richness of the real thing. Alright then, I could do this. Maybe not sell it, but I definitely could paint it.

I dabbed more paint onto the canvas, adjusting the colors for light and shadow and for mood. I worked to achieve the soft look of flesh over the firmness of bone, along with the intangibles like desire, uncertainty and excitement.

A knock on the door finally made me look up. When had the sky turned light? Paint splotches covered the previously white bathrobe robe. Too bad, I'd just have to buy them a new one.

"Coming," I said, looking over my work with amazement, and pride too. I grabbed up a cloth, flipping it over the canvas, careful to not smudge the paint.

Teros stood on the small porch, a covered tray in his hands. He looked at the paint covered robe. His eyes traced the deep V where it came together and the top of my breast peeked out.

That had to be my imagination. I pulled it tighter.

A smile lifted one corner of his mouth.

"I see you worked all night."

"Yeah, kind of. I guess I have to buy the monastery a new robe."

"Don't bother, they're used to it. Besides, getting the paint out of it won't be a problem." His eyes met mine.

You, getting me out of it, wouldn't be much of a problem either.

Geez, I really needed to stop thinking up this stuff.

"I brought you breakfast. Would you like me to put it inside?"

"Yes, sure."

I stepped aside letting him pass, eyes glued to the slide of that monk's robe over his firm bare ass. He set the tray down on the table and brought around the chair.

"Oatmeal, with brown sugar and blueberries which I picked myself this morning, coffee with enough cream for your cereal too, toast, orange juice, George squeezes it fresh, and bacon, crisp. Hope you like it."

"I'll love it. You should know that sandwich saved my life."

He laughed.

"When I'm working I generally don't eat very well. A handful of granola, a hardboiled egg, whatever my friends drop off is pretty much it."

He tsked. "You need energy to do your best work. I'll make sure you get everything you need while you're here."

His eyes went to the covered canvas. A twinge of embarrassment went through me.

"You don't have to show me if you'd rather not," he said as if he'd read my thoughts.

Before I could stop myself I walked over and whipped the cover from the painting. If Brother Teros got embarrassed by nudity or an expression of love this pure I would be sorry. But it felt important - no necessary- to show it to him. After all, if he was to be my helper, confidant and for all I knew, father confessor for the next three months, I needed to be sure he could handle the job.

Teros walked over and stopped in front of the painting. I watched him moving around it, tilting his head from side to side and looking at it from every possible angle, but not speaking.

"It's not finished," I said, unable to bear the silence. Not that it mattered; I had no intention of painting clothes on them.

"I haven't decided if I'm going to show it or not."

"This is —" he paused.

My heart slammed against my ribs. What if he hated it or worse disapproved?

"This is remarkable. It's really wonderful," Teros said finally. "How did you manage to capture them and everything I see in them in this one painting so quickly?"

"What is it you see? I mean, I think Danielle and May are great, even though I just met them. But beyond their obvious beauty, what else do you see?"

"Everything; I see their playfulness, love, cynicism, generosity and all of that youthful hope and exuberance that bubbles out of both of them in abundance."

"Youthful hope? Wow, you say that like you're so much older."

"Old is relative, wouldn't you say?" Teros eyes locked with mine and the black pupils in that sea of green flared.

He's not making a pass at me. Is he?

Teros left the painting to stand closer to me. Noticing the tiny pulsing of a vein at the base of his throat, I focused on it, afraid to continue the deep eye contact that could only lead me to making a complete idiot of myself.

"Do you think they'll mind?"

"How could they? You've made them look even more delightful than they already are."

Had he leaned infinitesimally closer? I stood frozen in place.

Teros finally broke the spell by walking over to pull the chair out from the table.

"You should eat before your breakfast gets cold."

I sat down and waited while he unfolded the linen napkin and placed it over my lap. Had I imagined it again, or had he snuck a peek down the opening of my robe. My hormones kick-started everything else, making my pussy wet and my nipples throb.

Hail Mary full of the grace. The Lord is with thee, blessed—

"Did you want coffee first?" Teros lifted the pot.

I nodded, grabbing the cream pitcher and adding a generous amount to the cup.

He lifted the metal lid off the oatmeal and toast, placing them on the table.

"Put the tray outside when you've finished. That way I won't bother you when I pick it up. "

"You're not bothering me."

He smiled again. "Good, I'll bring you lunch." Teros walked out, leaving me completely hot and bothered.

After nine and a half hours I no longer feared that the inspiration that allowed me to start this painting would desert me before I finished it. And I really needed a break from the intensity of this piece.

It felt good to abandon the paint covered robe for blue jeans, a gray Huskies sweatshirt and Birkenstock clogs. Despite Teros' assurances, I felt more than a little guilty stuffing the robe, paint, and all, into the clothes hamper. Grabbing a pencil and small sketch pad, I left the cottage.

Outside the sun shined, yesterday's storm forgotten except for the freshness in the air and the still-damp boughs that sprinkled moisture in the light breeze. I headed for the path to the beach between the cedars.

A steep slope led downward, but roughhewn steps of logs and gravel made the going easier. I jump-stepped from one platform to the next, splitting my attention between the spectacular view in the distance and the path ahead.

Three quarters of the way down, I heard someone chipping and scraping on wood. I followed the sound, leaving the steps, and crunching through fallen fir needles.

A massive tree trunk had washed onto the narrow pebble beach. I dodged around its tangled roots, splashing through the shallows. Ice cold water sloshed into my clogs. The sound changed to chopping and the smell of fresh cut cedar filled the air.

Now a large boulder stood between me and the sound. I skirted around it. Waves lapped at my feet. I stopped, frozen by the vision of him.

Bare-chested, Teros straddled a trunk working a chisel into the wood. He'd replaced the nut brown robe, with the dark green utility kilt of my dreams, and laced up hiking boots topped by a roll of thick wool socks.

I'd guessed right. He looked fantastic.

Teros turned around, a slow smile lighting his face.

"Serena."

I gulped in a breath, reminding myself he's a monk and I'm old enough to be his mother.

"Hi, I needed a break, but I didn't mean to interrupt."

"You're not interrupting." He stepped to one side revealing the emerging shape of a woman.

Although only half the face had been completed its beauty was mesmerizing. The wood came alive beneath his tools, the smooth curve of a cheek, an indulgent smile, and deep green eyes like his.

It's wood, stupid. How could you know the eyes were green? Somehow I did know. They were the same color as his. Maybe, before I left, I'd ask Teros to confirm it.

"She's beautiful."

"I thought I'd try for a new interpretation of Aphrodite."

"It's good. Do you mind if I take a closer look?"

His smile warmed me to the tips of my now frozen toes.

I plowed clumsily the rest of the way through the shallows.

"Of course not." Teros stepped to the side, letting me move next to the carving.

"You're no amateur woodcarver. This is really, really good."

"Glad you like it. It's been a long time since I've worked in wood. Lately it's been basalt and granite. I'd forgotten, there's something very…" He paused, as if searching for the word. "There's something incredibly…" His eyes sought out mine and a sexy smile lit his face. "Seductive about working with a live medium."

He's only talking about sculpting!

"There's more." Teros pointed toward the back.

I skirted the deadfall limbs that hadn't been trimmed away yet, and ducked under the long pointed root stems at the base of the tree. He'd begun to etch the goddess' body into the thick trunk section, a full swell of breasts, wide hips beneath a tiny waist wandered in and out the natural curves of the wood.

His eyes followed me. Suddenly my sweatshirt felt overwhelmingly hot, but I couldn't exactly take it off since I wasn't wearing anything underneath, not even a bra.

I reminded myself that Teros being a monk made it easier. No way could I compete with his ideal version of womanhood, no woman could.

"I'm going to get back to work, but you're welcome to stay," Teros said.

"Would you mind if I draw you, while you work?"

He shook his head, swinging a lock of black hair out of his eyes. "Not at all."

Taking a seat on a nearby rock, I flipped to a clean page and began to draw. From this vantage point I got a perfect view of his great legs, ripped stomach, strong arms, and perfectly muscled back. He climbed atop the tree to cut away a branch. Wow, he still wasn't wearing underwear. His was the body of one of those fabulous Greek statues.

Unable to stop myself, I let my thoughts wander to what it might be like to make love with a body that perfect. Would he be an equally perfect lover, giving as well as receiving or would I be left wanting?

Stop it! He's a monk!

Even though we didn't speak, I couldn't remember being more aware of anyone's presence in my entire life. Catching glimpses of his magnificent cock, every time he climbed over that log almost became routine. Okay not routine, but at least I stopped holding my breath each time it happened.

Finally he stopped, packed his chisels into a cloth bag and slid a black tee shirt over his head.

"I shouldn't have kept you here so long. You missed lunch," Teros said.

"I can miss a meal or two." I rose, patting my rounded belly. "Believe me, I wouldn't have missed this shot of inspiration for the world. Thank you."

The sun had slid low in the sky. A chilly breeze blew off the water, sending a shiver through me.

Teros stepped closer. Pulling a jacket from his bag, he wrapped it over my shoulders. I inhaled the heady mixture of male sweat and cedar resin.

"May I see it?" he asked.

For a moment I looked up at him confused, and then I remembered my sketch. The drawing I'd made confused me even more. Maybe I'd been inspired by his carving of Aphrodite, or maybe my subconscious had just been working overtime to conjure him up as the perfect Greek god.

In my drawing, his body rippled with power and raw sexuality. A barely restrained passion danced in his eyes along with an ethereal mixture of loneliness and seduction. Too much projection, hopefully he wouldn't notice.

The kilt became the soft folds of a short chiton and the laced-up hiking boots transformed into knee-laced sandals. A laurel crown sat upon his black hair.

I hadn't changed the setting. The choppy waters of Puget Sound and tall trees and rocky beach still surrounded him. But the wood chisel had become a short, curvy bow, with arrow nocked.

"Is this how you see me?" Teros asked.

I looked up, meeting his pleased expression. "I guess that's how I saw you a few moments ago. "

He looked puzzled, and then a smile lit his face.

My breath quickened and my heart beat sped up. My god, he's so gorgeous it almost hurts to look at him.

"Thank you. It's wonderful," he said.

A lump formed in my throat. "I should be thanking you. Honestly, when I stepped onto this island yesterday, I thought I'd never be able to draw again."

Teros shook his head. I watched, fascinated by the play of sunlight over his hair.

"All artists hit the wall every once in a while. This couldn't be your first time."

"I've had blocks before, but this is different. It didn't feel like a block. I felt cut off from the source."

I took a step away from him, putting some distance between me and my desire to sweep my fingers through his luxuriant hair.

"Something about this place is helping me to reconnect." I wasn't about to tell him what, or more to the point, who that was. "Is the offer still open to pose for me?" I asked. *Where had that come from?* "I mean—."

"I'd love to pose for you, if you'll return the favor."

"What? No, I mean—— look at me. I'm no Aphrodite."

He laughed, the deep sexy sound of it sending desire flooding through every cell of my body.

"No, you're not and believe me, for that I'm very glad. Serena, you are tempting in ways that you can't even see, but I can." He reached out, brushing a stray hair from my cheek.

Hail Mary, full of grace, please stop me from wanting this man so badly. I prayed silently.

"I'll pose for you, if you pose for me?" he asked.

He was so exquisite and so sexy; painting him might be as good as fucking him. Almost.

"How about only a bust?" I offered.

Tero's eyes went to where my breasts throbbed beneath the baggy sweatshirt. My nipples grew harder in response to his intense gaze.

"I'd be more than happy with only your bust," he said.

A mischievous look shined from his eyes as a smile curved his full lips.

Give me a break! Monks aren't supposed to flirt like this or look like him! It's not fair, like teasing a child with candy; or a menopausal woman with great sex.

"We have a deal then." I kept my voice deliberately light.

"I do my best work in the early morning." His tongue darted out, licking kissable lips.

"Will you meet me here tomorrow, around eight?"

"Okay, and I like to paint in the evening, so would you mind starting after dinner. I won't keep you up too late."

This could've passed for sexual banter if I wasn't fifty-eight and he wasn't thirty-something and a monk.

Oh well, I still looked forward to after dinner.

Chapter Four

Tonight I found an empty chair at the end of the table, across from the intense looking composer Richard Ware. He was talking to the woman sitting next to him. They grew silent as I pulled out my chair to take a seat. On my right sat an attractive, middle-aged, African-American man I hadn't seen the night before.

"I'm Serena Davies and I paint," I said, by way of introduction.

"Priscilla Lindquist, historian and writer," the woman said.

"Henry Goddard—"

"The novelist?" I asked.

He nodded. "The same."

"I absolutely fell in love with your last book, Songs of My Dreams."

"I appreciate that."

Danielle and May waved at me from the other end of the table. I waved back.

"What do you paint?" Richard asked.

"Landscapes mostly, but I'm open to anything that catches my interest."

"Ahh, I love Thomas Cole. That whole Hudson River School movement is so fascinating," Priscilla said.

I nodded and smiled. Whenever I said I painted landscapes, someone inevitably trotted out the Hudson River School like they were the last artists in the world to paint a decent landscape.

"My work is a bit more interpretive," I said. "Are you working on anything at the moment, Richard?"

"An opera," Richard said.

Priscilla added, "It's about the Battle of New Orleans during the Civil War, not 1812. I'm writing another book about the Civil War, more about the people than the war itself."

"Oh?"

"It's quite interesting really. Priscilla is remarkable." Richard said. "She stumbled across a fascinating first person account that I'm using as the jumping-off point for my opera."

Priscilla's complexion flushed an attractive pink, making me wonder if they might be consulting on more than history.

"It has all the right elements, love, betrayal, the tragic fall of the Great South," she said.

"Some folks didn't see the South as that great, or their fall as that tragic," Henry said, giving them a wry look.

"I'm sorry Henry, I wasn't meaning to imply." She turned bright red. "I meant within the context."

Henry's booming laughter rang out over the dining room. "I'm just kidding. Damn girl, you're just way too easy."

Teros and two monks I hadn't seen before entered with salad bowls. How many monks lived here? He leaned down, brushing against my shoulder as he deposited the bowl on the table next to me.

Did he have any clue how horny that made me? If only he'd just been a fatally attractive younger man, then I would find a way to make peace with my conscience for seducing him.

"Tonight George has prepared Caesar Salad, Salmon Trout Poached in Wine and Herbs, Potatoes Roasted with Rosemary and Sea Salt, and Coconut Flan for desert. George apologizes that this meal is not up to his usual standards and begs your indulgence and understanding." Teros said.

"He's got it. Let's eat," Henry said.

Laughter, and people began digging in.

I hadn't realized how hungry I was until the first fork full touched my tongue. Then I practically inhaled the fabulous food.

A fourth monk served the wine tonight, a buttery smooth Chardonnay. Between George's extraordinary culinary talents and the fascinating conversation of my table mates, my nervousness about later this evening didn't kick in until Teros came behind me with the tray of desserts.

"I'm stuffed. I think I'll pass," I said.

"I'll bring it with me and you can have it later if you'd like," Teros said.

My cheeks heated up and I looked around to see if anyone would make a big deal about it. Nobody appeared to notice or care.

Thankfully tonight there were no presentations or readings scheduled for after dinner, so I hurried back to my cottage, added some wood to the fire, moved the chair nearer the stove and repositioned the small lamp to cast a soft glow over him.

Next I fiddled with the canvas on the easel, honed the ends of a handful of charcoal pencils, dug out an eraser and soft brush. Then I went into bathroom and stood before the mirror.

He wouldn't think I'd done anything special if I pulled my unruly mass of hair on top of my head and unthreaded a few trailing tendrils. A little lipstick and mascara couldn't hurt either.

Finally a knock at the door put an end to all of my fussing. Teros stood on the small porch, a couple of covered dishes in his hands. I looked at the brown robe with disappointment. We hadn't discussed wardrobe, but I'd been hoping for at least the shirtless utility-kilt look or, even better, nothing at all. A secretive smile curved his mouth and made its way to his eyes, like he'd read the thought.

"Sandwich and your flan, I'll put them in the refrigerator unless you plan to eat dessert right away."

"No, let me do that. Please."

He stepped inside reluctantly handing me the dishes. His presence seemed to fill the room with heat, excitement and maleness.

I took the dishes and walked quickly to the refrigerator, anything to put some distance between us.

"You can take a seat in the chair by the stove, if you don't mind." Back to him, I crouched down to deposit the dishes in the small refrigerator and took a few breaths to rein in my raging lust.

"Did you want me seated any particular way?" His deep voice washed over me.

"No, I might reposition you later, but for now, sit however you're comfortable." I called over my shoulder unable, to turn and face him yet.

Okay. Enough! I would to have to turn around sometime. I heard the rustling of his robe and the creak of the chair as he settled into it. Schooling my features into a mask of professionalism, I rose slowly from the crouch and turned around.

All the oxygen rushed from the room, leaving me silently gasping like a fish. Blood boiled through my veins and speech left me completely.

Sitting sideways, Teros had draped his exquisite nude form with casual perfection in the chair. Heat and wetness flooded my pussy. Dreams do come true. Magnificent. Breathtaking. Gorgeous. I discarded every adjective that flew to mind as completely and totally inadequate to describe him.

Where golden olive skin met dark wood and ecru upholstery, a magical melding occurred in the dancing light of the fire. I now had a full unrestricted view of his huge cock. It lay draped across one muscular thigh, seemingly at rest, but still larger than life. I let my gaze wander over his form, taking in every angle and curve. Strength, without weakness, I'd never seen this before. Finally I looked into his eyes. Green fire burned deep within them.

The breath I'd been holding escaped me, jolting my heart into beating once again.

Get a grip girl, you've painted nude men before. At least I had in college. None of them had been this incredibly sexy. I should know because I'd fucked most of them too.

Teros smiled. "This is okay I hope."

"Yes, uh yes. You're perfect." I moved to the easel, trying to ignore the wetness, tingling, and the irresistible impulse to kneel and see how much of that great cock I could take into my mouth. Instead I picked up one of the pencils and forced myself to concentrate on capturing all the overwhelming virility and beauty in front of me.

Thankfully, the artist in me took over and my pencil flew across the canvas as I outlined the flawless curves and angles of his body that I would later paint. Teros sat absolutely still, his gaze somewhere in the corner of the room rather than on me, like he knew if looking into his eyes for more than a minute or two would send me over the edge.

Teros' contoured muscles beneath smooth olive skin were text book examples. But this gorgeous body also had a birthmark, in the shape of a lightning bolt, high on the left thigh and a scar above his right shoulder. Imperfections that only served to make him more perfect.

I stand when I work, which forces me to lean around the side of the canvas periodically, and also gave me brief respite from the waves of sensuality rolling off him. After a while I got to work on the details of that remarkable penis. I'd purposefully ignored it earlier, afraid the temptation would prove too much. But now I could see it as part of the whole, maybe the best part, or maybe not.

A twinge tightened my neck as I straightened up to grab a new pencil.

"Ouch!"

In an instant, Teros moved to my side, his strong fingers massaging the knotted muscles of my neck.

"You need a break," he said. Gently he pried the pencil from my fingers, which had also begun to cramp. How long had we been at this? The clock showed a quarter past midnight. I'd been at it over five hours.

"I'm so sorry. I didn't mean to keep you this long."

"Don't worry. I enjoyed watching you work. Now sit." Teros led me to the chair he'd been draped over a moment before. I settled into the cushions, still warm from his body.

"How about some chamomile tea with your sandwich? It will help you sleep."

He moved over by the refrigerator, dropping down on one knee, searching through a cabinet until he came up with an electric kettle and a canister. He still hadn't slipped on his robe. For this I thanked the gods.

Grace and power manifested in his every movement. He walked to the bathroom to fill the kettle, then returned and plugged it in. He retrieved cups from the cabinet and food from the refrigerator. I watched as he poured steaming hot water into the mugs. I was surprised when Teros unwrapped two sandwiches. He'd planned on working late.

"Here, drink this." Teros handed me a warm mug, watching me until I'd lifted it to my lips to sip.

My neck twinged again. Teros set his mug down on the table. Moving behind me, he slid his hand inside my shirt and gently gripped my knotted shoulders. His glorious naked body hovered over me while his hands soothed away the stiffness. Setting down my own mug, I gave myself up to his incredible ministrations, and my fantasy of what it would be like if this were only the prelude to a whole night of hot sex.

Suddenly he stopped, his fingers resting lightly on my clavicles. Electricity coursed through me, along with overpowering desire. This situation could get out of hand fast.

"Don't tighten up on me Serena," he said near my ear.

A moan slipped out before I could stop it.

"Teros, I need to be honest with you. I'm thinking and feeling things about you that are totally inappropriate not only because you're a monk. But I'm also old enough to be your mother and definitely should know better. I'm sorry. "

He kept massaging, but said nothing.

Talk about your awkward silences. The pressure of his fingers against my skin had me practically coming.

Nervous laughter. Mine.

"I'm sorry if I've embarrassed you. Maybe we should call it a night."

His breath tickled my ear. Then I felt his lips press against that sensitive spot just above my shoulder blade. A shudder went through me. I must be dreaming, either that or I'd just jumped onto the devil's expressway to hell.

He chuckled.

His hot breath against my skin made me wetter and my clit throb. I squeezed my legs tight.

This is freaking impossible!

He leaned over my shoulder, the heat from his chest penetrating the thin material of my top. I breathed in his scent and felt my pussy clinch reflexively.

His strong fingers slid under my chin and turned my face until only a few molecules of air separated our lips.

"Serena," he whispered. "I'm not a monk."

What!? Yes! No! Oh god help me!

Unable to stop I closed that space, putting my lips against his perfect mouth. He responded, burying his fingers in my hair and pulling me closer. After a brief chaste moment, his tongue slid into my mouth and it felt as if my body exploded to life.

Releasing my head his hands pulled me up from the chair, holding me against his hard body.

"I'm here to serve you," he said. Claiming my mouth again, Teros nipped my lower lip, sending a quiver through me. He tasted of cloves. His hand moved beneath my shirt, pushing aside the bra, and the callused tips of his fingers clamped down on my breast.

"Yes, oh my god yes," I said against his lips as he kneaded the breast. Then those rough hands slid lower over my stomach, waking every nerve ending into pleasure. I moaned, writhing against him.

He lowered his dark head to my chest, and burrowed under my shirt until he sucked one nipple into the heat of his mouth. The tip of his tongue swirled slowly around the areole, driving me crazy.

"Hmm," he murmured with a mouthful of my breast. "You taste even better than I thought you would." He slid his hands lower and teased their way past the waistband of my panties. His fingers curled into the coarse hair, but he stopped short of my throbbing clit. What is he waiting for?

Touch me there, damn it!

"I'm here to serve you. Tell me what you want," he said.

I couldn't say it. Even if he wasn't a monk, he was still too young. He kissed me again, this time teasing me with his tongue while the tips of his fingers moved a little lower, lightly tracing the sensitive ridge above my clit. I felt my knees go weak and his arm tighten around me.

The hardness of his cock pressed deep between my legs. I pressed back, feeling it jump.

Teros groaned, and cupped my pussy. I knew he felt it dripping and pulsing against his palm, betraying my hours of longing for him.

"Tell me what you want Serena."

You're being reckless and foolish, my good sense shouted.

I can stop after just a little more.

"Put your fingers inside me. Make me come, please."

Without a word Teros picked me up as if I weighed nothing, carrying me over to the couch. He stripped off my shirt, pants, and underwear. Then he placed one callused palm beneath my ass, lifting it up and spreading me wide. Bending down, he gently kissed my pussy. A flick of his tongue against my swollen clit and I felt myself coming. Those rough fingertips squeezed my ass hard, bringing me back to earth.

"Don't rush this," he said sternly. "Enjoy it."

I closed my eyes, loving the sweep of his soft hair against my thighs and the warmth of his breath as he exhaled into my pussy.

"I've waited for this, so now I'm going to take my time," he said.

His tongue slid along the ridge of my clit. My body jerked in response, slamming a knee into his nose.

"Ouch!" He jumped up holding his bruised nose.

"Oh my god, I'm so sorry! Let me see if there's some ice," I moved to get off the couch. His large hand held me in place.

"No damage done. But you're way too tense. We need to take care of that first."

Fucking him would certainly relax me, but it soon became obvious that wasn't what Teros had in mind.

Without another word he flipped my nude body over, straddled it, and began massaging my back.

"What makes you think this is going to calm me down? You know I can feel that extraordinary cock of yours pressing into me."

He chuckled, leaned down to kiss the back of my neck. "Shhh, just lie still."

Strong, skillful hands slid down the muscles of my back, easing out the tension. But they did nothing to stop the yearning I felt every time the tip of his cock brushed my leg. Long sensuous strokes started at the base of my skull, moved down my body to the bottoms of my feet and then he'd start over again.

Men generally didn't have the patience for this kind of thing, so I kept waiting for him to decide he wanted to get down to fucking. He didn't speak, didn't stop massaging. After a while I wondered if he'd changed his mind. God, I hoped not.

"Serena," he said sternly, his strong hands forcing me to relax again.

At some point I must've fallen asleep.

I woke in my bed beneath the covers.

"What the—"

I sat up with a start.

Teros laughed. "You fell asleep on me."

Outside the window the sun painted the sky with streaks of fuchsia. Teros came over to the bed wearing the monk's robe once again. Okay, so whatever had been between us last night had passed. Admittedly fucking Teros would likely prove another emotional complication that I couldn't afford. Besides, it wasn't a total loss. His excellent massage had loosened my muscles while providing me with enough masturbatory fantasies to last at least a year.

"I'm so sorry. I swear I've never fallen asleep while making love with a man, no matter how boring. — I'm sorry, I didn't mean you're boring— "

He laughed, slipped off the robe off and dropped onto the bed, next to me, covering my mouth with his. I gently sucked at his tongue in way of apology and he sucked back until our tongues battled for a few furious seconds.

Finally he conceded, pulling away.

"Now that you're rested and relaxed." He smiled, licking his lips and pushed me back against the pillows.

This time he really kissed me exploring every recess of my mouth while his hands played with my breasts until I thought I'd pass out from lust.

He ended the kiss, but kept his hands on my breasts, tracing outlines of the areoles with an unbearably light touch. "I'm here to serve you. Tell me what you want."

"Anything I want?" I asked, a surreal feeling washing over me. Frankly, no man had ever made this offer to me without the expectation of some future quid pro quo. Teros looked normal enough, but then again, most guys with unusual sexual proclivities looked normal. So was I really prepared to deal with that?

"No strings attached, promise," Teros said, again pulling the thought from my head.

"Okay, how about we take up where we left off?"

"I'd hoped that's what you'd want to do." His lips touched my neck and then began kissing a path downward. Distracted by the feel of his tongue tracing patterns against my chest, shoulder, breasts, the feel of two fingers easing into the slippery wet folds of my sex startled me.

"Relax, enjoy," he said. His thumb began making lazy circles over my clit, starting a flood. "Hmm, that's it Serena."

Teros fingers slid deeper into me.

This wouldn't last long if I didn't do something fast.

Reaching out, I wrapped my hand around that most gorgeous cock.

I reveled in the quiver that shook it. I held if for a few seconds, thick and pulsing in my hand and then I squeezed lightly, as I pulled my hand toward the head.

"Ahh." Teros arched into the pull. His fingers slid out until only the rough calloused tips remained inside my pussy. He buried them again, in and out with steady insistent pressure. I neared my climax,

This is such a bad idea!

All at once my body compressed, then blew open to the universe. The powerful orgasm overwhelmed my senses. Gripping Teros' cock like a lifeline, I clinched my pussy around his fingers and rode the wave.

When finally I stopped quivering, and returned to earth, he leaned down and kissed me.

"You are so beautiful when you orgasm, head thrown back, your hair like a bright red cloud. That's how I'd like to carve, you."

I laughed. "You're fantastic. Anything you want."

He smiled, a mischievous look coming into those deep peridot eyes.

"You can let go now."

"What?" I followed his glance down to where my hand still gripped his penis. "Oops, sorry, did I hurt you?" I released him, feeling like I'd broken an important connection.

"No."

Still erect, his cock stood tall between his muscular thighs. I'd wanted to feel that cock inside of me since that first fortuitous gust of wind. A glistening bead of pre-cum oozed from the tip. I looked up from it, meeting Teros steady green gaze.

"Anything?" I asked.

"Anything. I'm here to serve you."

"Then fuck me, please."

"Gladly." He reached into the night table drawer and pulled out a condom.

"Let me." I took the foil packet as I reached for his cock. It seemed to tilt toward my hand, meeting me half way. I leaned down, swirling my tongue around the head. Teros groaned, full lips pulling back from perfect teeth in a pleasure grimace. I'd barely finished unrolling the condom over his length when he grabbed me around the waist and pulled me onto his thighs. Lifting my butt, he seated me onto his penis.

Large, hot, and pulsing, I felt a twinge as my pussy stretched to accommodate his size. Releasing my ass, he cradled my breasts in his palms, using them to hold me in place.

Slowly he pushed deeper inside, then pulled back. Each stroke he went deeper, unlike anything I'd ever experienced. God he felt good. I held my breaths, thought about painting, counted backwards from one hundred, trying to hold out and make it last longer, when all I wanted to do was bounce up and down on his cock, screaming yes, yes, yes like a porn star.

Teros, on the other hand, adopted a leisurely pace, sliding in and out of me with a delicious steady rhythm as if he could do this forever. Unable to hold back any longer I began rocking back and forth, forcing his cock deeper.

"That's it," he whispered. One hand left my breasts to take my clit between his fingers. He rolled the tip between thumb and forefinger like a glass bead.

I continued rocking slowly letting each stroke penetrate me fully. Teros murmured his pleasure.

"Yes, that's perfect," he whispered. He closed his eyes letting his head loll back. I kissed the column of his neck, loving the feel of it vibrate as he growled his pleasure.

It took me a while to realize that he wouldn't come until I did.

I couldn't hold out any longer. My breathing grew quick and shallow.

"Oh yes, please, please," I said.

"Shhh, let it happen," he said.

Light, colors, and heat flooded me in a psychedelic storm. My body tightened and exploded into an orgasmic universe. His skin grew hot beneath my fingers.

Raising us both higher, Teros drove into me, pushing me toward another climax. I watched him come. Suddenly his eyes opened and locked onto mine and I could swear something in those green depths glowed to life. Then my third orgasm hit, knocking the breath from me and focused all my attention on his cock.

Wave after wave of pleasure wracked my body.

A stream of foreign words poured from Teros before he buried his own scream in the hollow my throat.

I'd had friends tell me about fucks so good they swore they saw god. I understood that now.

We lay spooned together, watching the sky grow brighter. Teros planted a string of kisses on my shoulder. He whispered loving words I didn't understand.

"What are you saying?"

"It's Greek. I'm saying I am now in heaven."

I kissed him.

"I'd love to lay here with you forever, but I've got to help with breakfast."

I groaned pushing my butt against his crotch. His penis sprang up between my legs.

"Can't the others handle it?" I asked, wanting feel him inside me again.

"Yes, but I said I would help. Besides, you have to get ready to pose for me. So I can carve your bust." He gave my breast a playful squeeze.

"Alright, I'll let you go."

He kissed me again, and climbed from the bed. I rolled over to watch him drop the brown robe over his head. Handy garment, I should get one.

"Would you have stayed if I said I wanted you to?"

"Of course, I'm here to serve you. I should go now, unless—" He let that trail off, but the glint in his eyes made the rest of his thought clear. I wriggled unconsciously at the thought of having him again.

"You're going to have to tell me more about this service you provide. Like why you're here, if you're not a monk."

"It's a long story. I'll tell you about it later. If you want to know anything from me Serena, all you have to do is ask."

"Was it good for you?" I blurted out. *Where the hell had that come from?*

His eyes locked with mine.

"You know the effect you have on men."

What? Embarrassed, I tried to look away, but those eyes held me enthralled.

"You don't?" He looked incredulous. "Then let me tell you the effect you have on me." He bent down, coming nose to nose with me. "When my cock is buried inside you, I feel like the world is an absolutely perfect place. Fucking you, Serena Davies, is a totally mind blowing, fantastic experience that I plan to enjoy a whole lot more of. That is if you'll let me."

"Good, I mean yes," I said, feeling myself blush.

"Good. Did you want me to bring you breakfast?"

"No. I'll come to the hall. I love to watch you serve."

The monastery served breakfast buffet-style. A large tray of fresh fruit, cereal, pitchers of milk and orange juice, and with a toaster oven with baskets of fragrant breads, sat on a table in the corner. The sideboard held covered chafing dishes. I lifted the lids of each: fluffy scrambled eggs, bacon and sausage, thick cut oatmeal and a hash made with smoked salmon and potatoes.

I grabbed a bowl of oatmeal with raisins and a generous amount of cream. Danielle and May were the only other people in the dining room, so I joined them.

At some point I needed to show them the painting and get their approval to include it in my gallery opening. I wanted to make sure they knew I wouldn't display it if either of them objected.

"Good morning," I said.

"Morning," Danielle answered. "You look all glowy. Don't tell me you got some."

Right then Teros came into the room, the corners of his mouth pulling into a big grin when his eyes rested on me.

"Oh yeah, I'd say she hit that," May said. "Good for you. That man is almost enough to make me think about going hetero."

"How's the writing coming," I asked.

May's smile faded. "Not so good. You know, folks only come here when it's not working for them. The healing powers of St. Cat's breaks through the block. At least that's what they say."

"How long have the two of you been here?"

"Almost two months and no revelations yet," May said.

"I keep telling her it'll happen." Danielle reached over to squeezing her partner's hand.

I took a banana from the bowl on the table.

"When you're writing erotic literature it's hard to keep bringing something fresh to the table. I've written sixteen erotic bestsellers in three years and I'm tapped out. There only so many ways to fuck and I've put together combos that have literally landed people who tried them in traction. Name the place, the way, the time of day, the position, toys, kinks, tools, and I've done it."

"I agree with Danielle, it will come, sometimes sooner, sometimes later."

"So how's it coming for you?" May winked. "No pun intended."

"Good. No, great actually."

Teros leaned down to refill my coffee cup.

"Good morning, Teros," May and Danielle said in unison. "Sleep well?"

"Yes. How about you two?"

"Good. No great actually," Danielle said and cracked up. May joined in.

Teros' smiled at them with such intensity both women went silent.

"Thank you for asking," he said, and took their empty plates.

"Wow!" Danielle said. "What is it about him?"

May looked up from her cup. "Did your breakthrough happen?" she asked.

"Actually it did, and I wanted to talk to you both about it. You know I've painted landscapes and still-lifes for my entire career. But ever since I stepped off that boat I've had the urge to paint people."

Danielle and May looked at each other. "Teros," they said.

I could feel the blush warming my face. "It's not just him. It's everybody. It's like stepping out of my comfort zone has forced me to draw on something deeper. Some wellspring I didn't even know I had."

"You might be on to something." May took a bite of her roll. "Maybe I should try writing something that isn't erotic, just to get past the barrier."

"It can't hurt." Danielle said.

Finally I worked up the nerve to ask them.

"I've started a new piece. It's of the both of you and I'd like to include it in my show, but only if neither of you would mind."

"You painted us?" Excitement lit Danielle's face. "When do we get to see it?"

"It's not finished yet, but how about tonight after dinner?"

"Tonight it is. I can hardly wait," Danielle said.

"Will Mr. Gorgeous be there?" May asked.

"Don't know. Hope so." I glanced down at my watch. It read twenty to eight. "Gotta get back to work. See you at dinner?"

"Sure, we'll save you a seat."

Back in my cabin, I applied light coats of lipstick and mascara and twisted my hair, pinning on top of my head. Hopefully it would give me that long necked Grecian look, while minimizing my impending double chin. Enough primping. He'd seen my morning face already and it really didn't get much worse than that. Besides I didn't want to keep him waiting. I grabbed my sketch pad and a jacket.

Chapter Five

Half way down the path to the beach the whine of a chainsaw tore into the quiet. I thought of Teros in his utility kilt and ran the rest of the way. He stood wide-legged and bare-chested, wielding a chainsaw to remove the remaining limbs from a stump. He bent over to pull away a twig. Nope, still no underwear. A wave of lust went through me.

Teros looked up as I scrambled over the rocks. Turning off the chainsaw, he set it down and closed the space between us.

His arms encircled me, sketch pad and all. His lips covered mine. I welcomed the intrusion of his tongue and pressed my breasts against his sawdust covered chest and my pelvis against the erection lifting the heavy canvas fabric of the kilt.

"Hmm." I murmured as his hand massaged my nipple through the shirt.

I reached down to wrap my fingers around his penis. He got harder, pressing his length into my hand.

"How about a quickie to take the edge off?" I suggested.

I didn't have to ask a second time. Teros pushed down my pants. He reached into one of the many handy pockets of his kilt and pulled out a condom. He ripped the foil, rolled it down his length and backed me against a tree. I wrapped my legs around his waist, feeling rough bark press into the flesh of my ass. I'd probably be digging splinters out for a week. Totally worth it. A crooked smile on his face and his pupil flared as his slid two fingers inside me for a second.

"I love it when you're wet and ready for me." The tip of his penis teased at my opening making me frantic. I moved against it, scraping my butt over the rough tree bark. Suddenly I heard voices on the pathway. Teros froze.

"Don't stop now. I can't" I whimpered.

Teros drove the full length of himself inside of me with one powerful stroke. Pulled out and pushed in again. I pushed back, loving the delicious pain of a big cock, eager to come before we got interrupted. Using those strong thighs he pumped in and out of me.

"Come on," I urged him toward climax.

My pussy clenched convulsively. So close. His hot breath fanned my neck.

I felt the scream building in my throat. "Put your fingers in my mouth," I said on a ragged breath.

He didn't ask why, he just did it. I suckled them, tasting the saltiness of my own pussy and the bitter sweetness of tree pitch. I tried not to bite down as I came hard, wave after wave shuddering through me.

The voices grew closer. Teros grunted twice, thrust deep into me, and shot his load. His body quaked against mine, sending a bolt of desire to the core of my being. Staring silently into each other's eyes we both came again in one brief forceful wave.

Finally spent I slumped against his broad chest. He still gripped my ass with both hands. One finger moved against the tight bud of my anus. Was I imagining the speculative look he gave me? Had he tried the pleasures of anal, or could I teach him this?

They were right above us when the uncontrollable urge to giggle hit me. Pressing my lips tightly I looked helplessly at Teros, who pasted his lips over mine and shoved his cock in until it filled me up.

Henry and Priscilla seemed oblivious to everything except each other. We watched them head down the beach in the other direction.

When they'd gone Teros whispered, "Since we're here." He began sliding in and out of me with long luxurious strokes until I came a third time. Three seemed to be his number. I couldn't complain. He extricated himself, the kilt dropping back into place. Maybe I should get one of those too, so much easier, I thought as he leaned down to kiss my pussy before pulling my panties and pants up.

"Hmm, you are the most delicious woman, Serena Davies."

"And you leave me without words. Promise me we'll do more quickies," I said.

He laughed at that, moving over to where he'd been working when I arrived.

"I found this chunk of redwood washed up on the beach a few months ago. It either worked its way up the coast, or fell off a barge. At any rate, it seemed like destiny that I would use it to produce something very special."

I watched his back muscles flex as he hoisted the huge round of wood atop the stump he'd been trimming. Stripped of its bark, it must've weighed close to two hundred pounds.

Teros went over to his bag and pulled out a folding stool.

"This will be more comfortable than that rock." He unfolded it for me.

I retrieved my crushed sketch pad from the base of the tree and noticed Teros had done more work on the Aphrodite. The long curve of her neck and the beginning swells for breast were much further along. Talented, considerate, and quite possibly the best fuck I'd ever had. So why did he have to be so young?

"Will it bother you if I start another drawing of you?" I asked as I settled into the chair.

"Not at all." He looked at me, lifting his eyebrows.

"What?" I asked.

"No top, please. I want to carve your beautiful breasts."

"But—"

Teros pulled a jacket from his bag and tossed it to me. "In case you get cold," he said. The look of lust in his eyes had me wet and wanting again. "No top."

I pulled off my shirt. He nodded and began digging at the wood with a large chisel.

I retreated into my own world, sketching him; chisel in hand, trees at his back. If he wasn't a monk, why was he here? And how old was he?

"I'm a lot older than I look," he said absently as he walked around the stump.

"How did you know that's what I was thinking?"

"I can see the worry on your face and because it's what you've been thinking about since we first laid eyes on each other. Believe me, I'm not concerned about your age."

"So how long have you been a sculptor?"

"Nice try, a long time. I also teach. Anything else you want to know?"

"Is Teros your full name or is it short for something?"

"It's short for Anteros. I'm Greek. I think your work is some of the most exceptional and evocative I've ever seen. I've always known how old you are and I wanted to fuck you even before you stepped green-faced off that tugboat, wearing that detestable rain hat. Is all of that clear?" Amusement, mixed with passion burned in that hard green stare.

I dropped my gaze back to my sketch pad. "Yes, I think that's all I need for right now."

Teros was right. Why was I being so prudish about the age difference? We were on an island and this was a summer fling. We weren't planning the rest of our lives together.

"On second thought I do have one more question."

He set down his chisel, crossing his arms over the hard planes of his stomach.

"What?"

"Are you the only one not wearing underwear or do the monks all go au naturel?"

"Well, I can't say I've actually looked."

His mouth turned up into a smile and desire ignited behind his eyes. "But I chose not to wear any because I thought it might help me get you into bed."

Stunned into silence, I stared down at my sketch pad and concentrated on the sound of Teros' chisel digging into the wood.

"Ready for a break?" Teros asked.

I looked down at the sketch of him, surprised I'd actually managed to focus on my work, rather than on my rampant desire.

"I brought some bread, cheese, a bottle of the monastery's own wine and a poached pear salad from George. We can share lunch here or you can go back up to the hall."

"I'd love to eat here, with you." I pulled Teros jacket on and zipped it up. "Forgive me. I don't know what got into me. I guess I've seen too many of those National Enquirer covers, older woman dissed by younger man, headlines."

He looked puzzled.

"Not that the Enquirer even knows I exist. You know what I mean."

He opened the container of pear salad and spooned some into a paper cup, passing it to me. "Would it matter if they did?"

"No, I guess not. Did George send a note apologizing for the salad?"

"No, but he probably would've if he'd known I'd taken some. He's getting better though. Really, he used to come out and do a ten minute apology himself."

"Well then, I'd say letting someone else do it is an improvement."

Priscilla and Henry headed back up the path. This time they saw us.

"Hey Teros, mind if we look at what you're doing?" Henry asked.

Priscilla seemed busy trying to redo the buttons on her blouse.

"No, come on over. Can I offer you two some wine or food? We've got plenty." Teros pulled a couple more paper cups from his bag.

"No, thank you we're going back for lunch."

Priscilla finally joined the group. I reached up, plucking a twig from her hair.

"Thank you," she said. Joining Henry, she circled the sculptures, stopping to glance back at me. "These are beautiful, both of them."

"I know one of them is Ms. Davies, who is the other?"

"Aphrodite." Teros said.

"Ah yes, goddess of love, beauty and sex, wife of Hephaestus, lover of Ares and mother to Eros and his brother Anteros to whom she passed on her sexual prowess," Henry said.

Teros looked uncomfortable for a second.

"You know your mythology."

"Thanks for letting us look. We'd better hurry, don't want to miss whatever special treat George is sorry for at lunch. We'll see you later."

Priscilla grabbed Henry's hand and pulled him toward the path.

I waited until they were out of earshot.

"Don't tell me Henry and Priscilla are knocking boots. I thought she was collaborating with Richard."

Teros raised one thick eyebrow quizzically.

"Knocking boots?"

"Having sex," I explained.

"Oh, I get it."

He laughed quietly to himself, while I wondered if this was one of those generation gap indicators.

"They each have something the other needs. Sex can be one of the fastest paths to figuring out what that is, or one of the most destructive."

"Sculptor and philosopher?"

"Not really. I've seen it work both ways." He passed the bread and a pot of soft cheese along with a spreader.

"So which path are we on?"

"I guess we'll find that out, if you're willing."

"Definitely, at least for now. But I'm sorry, I do have one last question."

Teros looked at me with mock exasperation. "What is it?"

"How did you end up working here?"

"I came here, the first time almost two years ago, after running headlong into that block we talked about. I stayed six months. The monks here took care of me and gave me the space and solitude to regain myself. I promised I'd repay them in some way. So I volunteer during the summer helping other artists find their way."

"Sculptor, philosopher and saint."

He shook his head, disagreeing. "You know how you rolled in here running on empty? Well, that was me. Brother Joshua, the head of the order, loaned me this book of paintings. He said he wasn't sure if it would help, but it had helped him.

At first I couldn't believe someone could produce such emotionally challenging work. Over the course of six months, I looked through that book at least once every day and every day I found something different to make me sigh, or laugh, or just glad to be alive. Those paintings filled up that empty spot inside me." Teros expression softened. "They were your paintings, Serena."

The bread I'd swallowed stopped at the lump in my throat. I coughed. He handed me a cup of wine to wash it down.

"Wow, you put a lot on a woman," I said when I could speak again.

"I don't mean to."

I looked away training my gaze on the light sparkling on the Sound.

We worked in silence until Teros started to pack up his chisels. I approached the bust. I was surprised by how far he'd gotten.

He'd piled my hair on top of my head which accentuated the long graceful neck, minus the skin pouches that had shown up sometime around my forty-second birthday. Beneath the mass of wooden curls, I could see the beginnings of a face far too beautiful to be mine, with wide eyes and high cheek bones and a luscious mouth.

"It's gorgeous, but that isn't me."

"Of course it's you, though I don't think I did you justice."

I planted a big, wet, sloppy one on his full lips.

"It's perfect. I love it."

He actually blushed. "I'm glad it pleases you. I've got to get cleaned up to serve. None of the others deliver George's apology the way he likes it done.

"Then by all means, don't wait for me. I'm going to sit here a while and sketch the sunset. "

He slung the bag over his shoulder and kissed me hard. "I'll try to skip the dishes so I can come over earlier. Take this, in case it gets too dark to see your way back up." Teros handed me a flashlight.

"Whenever you get there, I'll be waiting. Oh yeah, I've invited May and Danielle over to look at their painting."

"Hope they don't stay long. We've got boots to knock." He laughed and kissed me again before heading up the path. I watched his strong legs taking the makeshift steps two at a time and that kilt riding up in the back beneath his bag, showing off his perfect tight ass. I should tell him about that.

Nah!

The excellent meal of baby lettuce salad, grilled duck breasts with Grand Mariner orange sauce, and steamed polenta with sundried tomatoes, started with an apology and ended with huckleberry cheesecake. Teros didn't bother to serve my desert. He'd bring it with him.

Wine bottles were passed, people talked, and actually shared their work. Teros and I shared smiles and the occasional quick feel. And we weren't the only ones touching. A euphoric May couldn't keep her hands off Danielle as she told everyone about her breakthrough.

"And I owe it all to Serena. She gave me this great idea to write something different. So I went back to my first love in writing," May said.

"What was that?" Richard asked.

"Mysteries. I didn't make nearly as much money at it, but I really loved twisting a plot together, leaving clues, and dropping red herrings. My first book received a Shamus Awards nomination. "

"So should I expect to see a new May Ngyuen mystery coming out soon?" I asked.

"Hell no, I told you they don't pay worth crap. Besides, I have two books left on a five book deal. But you can expect to see a new May Ngyuen erotic mystery coming to your local bookseller."

Everyone began leaving the table and heading toward the piano in the conversation area. Danielle and May looped their arms through mine on either side and guided me toward the door.

"Richard is playing part of his opera tonight. He's great." May said.

"And really, really long," Danielle said. "So we told him you'd invited us first to view a new painting. Hope you don't mind, but we'll probably look and run. We've got some research to do," Danielle said.

She looked at me and winked. "You can join us if you'd like."

"I'm a little old to change teams, but one never knows."

"Oh well, we can hope," May said. "You're actually one very sexy old broad." Her face grew red. "Oops I'm sorry, I didn't mean to call you old. Really, I meant it as a compliment. I mean obviously Teros thinks — Oops, sorry. "

"When you dig your foot out of your mouth May, I've got something else you can put in it." Danielle licked her lips suggestively.

We stopped in front of my cabin door.

"Come on in, I don't want to hold you ladies up from important matters."

"Besides you've got business of your own" May said.

"You're right about that."

We stepped into the living room. Teros had started the stove. The warmth felt welcome after the walk over. He'd also placed the five foot canvas of May and Danielle on the easel, covered.

"First let me say I'm not a voyeur, this comes straight from my imagination. I'd like to be able to display this in my upcoming show, but I won't if you're embarrassed or offended."

"So show us already," May said.

With a shaking hand I carefully pulled the cover off. The smell of acrylic paint wafted off the canvas.

"It's not finished yet."

They both stared, wide eyed, mouths hanging open.

Danielle's mouth closed, then opened again. She tried to speak and started coughing.

"Here, let me get you something to drink."

Teros had put the rest of our lunchtime wine in the refrigerator. I set it on the counter and bent down to the cupboard to get glasses. When I stood back up, Danielle and May were drinking straight from the bottle, passing it back and forth.

"Holy shit, this is so fucking beautiful," May said.

"Wow, wow, wow. You are damned good," Danielle added.

"So, you don't mind? I mean I didn't peek in your window or anything and you both seemed pretty open about your sexuality. What can I say, it just came to me? "

"Hey, I know you didn't peek in the window because I don't look that good. How could anyone be offended by something so completely awesome? "

May leaned over to take Danielle's face between her palms. She pressed her cherry, heart shaped mouth to Danielle's. Then, mouths fully open, they kissed, tongues engaged. A wave of lust heated me up.

"Sorry about that, but your painting made me remember why and how much I love this woman." May had tears in her eyes. "Thank you, again."

"And it made me think just how much I want to make love to this woman."

Danielle handed me the now empty wine bottle.

"We'll bring the next one," she said.

"We'd be honored if you put it in your show," May called over her shoulder as they hurried out the door, already tearing at each other's clothes. I hoped they'd make it back to one of their cottages before the main event.

Setting aside their canvas, I placed Teros back on the easel and went to work. No color had been added, but I didn't need it to see the green of his eyes, the blue black of his hair, or the golden olive of his skin.

I tried desperately to forget what Teros had told me about what my paintings meant to him. But it refused to go away, rolling around in my brain and carving a pathway to my heart.

Keep it light. You definitely don't need another emotional disaster and he's too young to want to hang around long.

I picked up the charcoal and began working the details of his face. His nose was long and straight. Some might have said a hair too large, but with people, like landscapes, the beauty didn't lie in the parts, but in the composition.

When he looked at me from beneath heavy lids, it felt like he saw me naked, and liked what he saw.

Eyes again, damn it. No way could I capture all the warmth, humor, compassion and passion in Teros eyes. I'm not sure if anyone's talent could meet that challenge. But the way a smile lifted his cheeks unevenly and dimpled one side would make the heart of any mortal woman skip a beat. And that I could do.

A few sweeping strokes from his hairline to behind, his ear that dark-as-a raven's-wing hair came to life, blown by a slight, unseen breeze. Thick with muscular cords, I worked on the column of his neck, adding the adorable bump of Adam's apple I'd missed last night. You can't remember everything when your body's screaming for sexual release. Somebody should put that in a fortune cookie.

Finally he knocked on the door. I ran to open it. Teros grabbed me up in his arms, planted his lips on mine, and carried me to the bedroom. He set me down and jerked his robe off.

The first time would be another quickie. This suited me fine since painting him had worked up quite a need.

"Serena."

He whispered my name and pulled the shirt over my head. He took my breast in his mouth, bra and all, while his hands tugged at my pants.

"All I could think about is you. You're lucky I didn't take you right there on the dinner table."

"Oh yeah, and you've got to start wearing something under that robe. I nearly went crazy, especially when you pressed your cock against my back."

He laughed, sliding his fingers into me.

"I thought you'd like that. Hmm, feels like you're ready too."

"Top."

"What?"

Naked and entwined we were backing toward the bed.

"I'm calling the top position."

"Whatever you wish. I'm here to serve you."

"That's right. You are. And after you've taken care of this aching between my legs, we'll talk about how else you can do that." I said, straddling his narrow hips and easing down onto his erect cock.

My body lit up like I'd plugged in.

Chapter Six

Sated, I collapsed onto Teros chest. He wriggled his penis still buried in me.

"I apologize that the first fuck did not meet my usual standards and beg your understanding and indulgence," he said with mock seriousness.

"Umm, don't worry about it. I'll tell you when you're not doing it right."

I paused, still unsure of how to broach the subject of trying something different.

"Tell me, how do you feel about the pleasures of backdoor sex?"

I watched his face, hoping that his finger playing with my anus when we'd fucked hadn't been an accident.

"You have such a lovely, tight feeling anus. I actually dreamed about being in it last night."

"Well you should've said something this morning, because we both could've saved a few fantasy hours."

"Anticipation only serves to sharpen pleasure."

I slid off his cock, stripped off the condom and stretched on a new one. I also grabbed the tube of lubricant from the drawer, slathering a large dollop.

I watched a smile spread across his face and his eyes burned even brighter. Turning away, I dropped to my elbows.

I heard his sharp intake of breath. His hands gripped my hips on either side. His lips kissing each butt cheek. I squirmed, anxious to have him begin. His teeth sunk into my tender flesh.

Serving Serena

"Don't rush me, I want you to enjoy this as much as I will. And by the way you have an absolutely delectable ass."

"Okay, flattery will get you everything."

Teros kissed the other cheek, slid his fingers into my anus, spreading the lubrication. I clamped down while he moved them in and out, easing me toward another orgasm. After a few moments I felt his penis probe at the opening to my ass. Anxious to feel that delicious initial entry, I pushed back hard against him, down his length until it filled me up.

He gasped, "Yes!" His hand grasped my hips holding me steady and settling me further onto his cock.

Oh my god, I'd never taken a man as large as him back there. I adjusted to ease the fullness. Every nerve ending ignited. Then he began, in and out, slowly, carefully, as if he didn't want me to miss a single exquisite sensation. His hot hands gripped my hips, guiding me through the perfect rhythm. My breathing quickened.

I adored a good ass fucking and Teros had perfected the technique, like everything else he did. How could I possibly think I'd have anything to teach him, anything at all?

His breath blew hot across my back. "Gods, I love to fuck you," he said. "I could do this forever."

"I don't thinks so because I'm about to come,' I panted. Without my needing to ask he slid his hand back between my legs and began working my clit.

"Oh my god! Oh my god! Oh!"

I thought this climax would kill me for sure. I stopped breathing as the blood abandoned my brain and rushed to feed the action.

Teros kept driving his great big cock into my rear while those wonderful callused fingers tweaked my clit until I finally stopped coming.

It still surprised me that he would grow even bigger right before he came. Inside the tight confines of my anus, I felt as if he'd split me wide open and I didn't care. Finally he roared and began pumping his seed. His hot balls slapped against my butt. The feel of his cum flowing hot and tingly into the condom made me orgasm again.

Exhausted, we collapsed.

Teros filled two glasses from the pitcher beside the bed, passing me one.

"No need to apologize for that," I said.

"Hmm, it was rather good, wasn't it?"

Reaching over, I smacked him upside the head with the pillow, and for that he kissed me. Then he slipped from bed and headed to the bathroom.

Oh-mi god I could watch that ass forever. Wrong, just for two months and 22 days more.

After a few moments I heard the water running into the bathtub. Teros came out carrying a robe for me.

"I'm drawing us a bath," he said.

"Nice. But that tub's pretty small."

"We'll manage." A feral smile lit his face.

Several delightful hours passed in the tub. When we finally climbed out, Teros looked delicious. I, on the other hand, was reminded why women my age shouldn't spend long hours in water. Because we come out looking like raisins.

He wrapped a towel around me and began to dry.

"I'm sorry that I'm keeping you from working. I know how important this show is to you. "

How had he known about my show? I hadn't told him. But I had told Brother Joshua when I begged to be allowed to come without the usual reservation, interview, or waiting list.

"I'm not sorry." I rubbed myself against the planes of his chest. "Not even a little bit."

Teros laughed.

"Well you're going to have plenty of opportunity to work because I'll be off island all day tomorrow buying supplies for the monastery."

"Oh?" I couldn't keep the disappointment out of my voice. How had I managed to become so attached, after only a few days?

"Don't worry; I'm going to miss you even more. But I also want to see some work when I return."

"And if you don't?"

"If I don't see enough progress, Serena Davies, I'm gonna have to cut you off. Ouch!" he jumped as my teeth closed on his nipple.

Grasping my butt Teros lifted me until I could feel his penis pushing at my crotch.

"What makes you think I won't cut you off?" I asked, pulling away.

"Because you can't."

His face smiled, but his serious tone belied it.

Did he know? I had been trying to convince myself I couldn't be in love with him after such a short time. Were my feelings for him so obvious?

"And what makes you think that I can't?" I asked.

I held breath as the silence stretched out forever. I watched his expression, looking for a clue. Would he actually give me a serious answer? Oh god, I hoped not.

His lips pulled into a grin.

"Because you can't get enough of this hot monkey love."

Okay, yes, so he's like any other man, totally oblivious and completely conceited about his sexual prowess. Although in his case, he had a lot to be conceited about. I can live with that. It isn't like any of this would last.

He pulled me close again. I looked up into that beautiful face and for an instant I glimpsed something, ancient, powerful. A bolt of fear shot straight through my soul. Then the look disappeared.

When I awoke the next morning, Teros was gone, but a bright bouquet of wild flowers lay where his head had been. I put the flowers in a glass of water and dressed for breakfast.

For some reason I found myself unable to wipe the grin off my face, even after May gave me a loud wolf whistle.

"Hey, don't you remember what your mother warned you about when you were a little girl?" Danielle asked.

"My mother warned me about a lot of things."

"Then she probably told you if you don't stop grinning so hard, your face is going to stick that way. Uh oh, it already has," May teased.

I grabbed cereal and coffee and took a seat at the table. Priscilla and Henry came over and sat down next to me.

"May and Danielle have been raving to everyone about the fabulous painting of them you did," Priscilla said. "We'd love to see it."

"Sure, if it's okay with them."

I looked across the table at the two women for permission.

"Hey, we want the whole world to see it," Danielle said.

"In that case you're welcome to come over after breakfast."

"Great, we'll leave you to eat then." Henry said. He wrapped an arm around Priscilla's slim waist and they sauntered off.

Richard leaned over. "May I come to the showing, too?"

"Sure, why not?" I said.

By the time I'd finished breakfast, all of the artists- in-residence and a couple of the monks had asked to join the party.

When I dropped my dishes off at the window to the kitchen, a hand reached out lightly touching my wrist. Part stooping, part kneeling, I got my eyes down to the opening. All I saw is a blue apron.

"I want to apologize for the lumps in the oatmeal." The deep baritone voice belonging to the apron said. "Tomorrow it should be better."

"The oatmeal tasted delicious, George."

"Thank you. Everyone is talking about your painting of May and Danielle. Would you mind if I came to see it too?"

"Not at all George. I'd love to have you see it. There should be quite a crowd after breakfast."

"May I come at another time? I mean I'll put pants and a shirt on, but I'd rather see it with less people around."

I tried not to gasp as I suddenly realized the implication of what he'd said. The only thing he had on now was the blue apron.

"Come any time. I'll be working all day in my cottage."

"With Teros gone and all," he added helpfully.

"Yeah, with Teros gone." Does everyone know I am screwing Teros? "I'll see you then. I'm glad to finally meet you and I think your meals are fabulous."

"Thank you Ms. Davies. That means a lot, coming from an artist of your caliber."

"Call me Serena. That would mean a lot to me coming from a chef of your caliber."

Chapter Seven

This might be more people than would show up at the gallery opening, I thought as I made my way through the crowd of a dozen or so, almost the entire population of the island.

"We heard you've done some drawings of Teros. Can we see those too?"

They were certainly a well-informed group.

"Sure give me a minute to set them up." I went into the cottage, picked up my robe, buried the used condoms in the waste can in the bathroom, and straightened the quilt on the bed before setting up the two paintings underway. The painting of May and Danielle, I put on the easel and moved it near the back of the room. Teros I placed on the chair by the window. The charcoal and pastel drawings I laid out on the table. Last I pushed the couch against the wall to make more space and opened the door to let in the critics.

At first, no one spoke a word as everyone crowded around the painting of May and Danielle. Then suddenly they were all talking at once, throwing around adjectives like: soulful, beautiful, and a masterpiece.

"What'd we tell you, completely off the chain, right?" Danielle announced. Voices rose in agreement.

Priscilla came over and stood next to me. "I know I'm not as beautiful as our poet and our erotic author, but if you need more models, I'd be honored," she said quietly. Small room, everyone heard her and "Me too's, "rang out.

Finally they turned their attention to the painting of Teros. The women drew in a collective breath, forming a worshipful circle around it.

"Is all of that real or is it Memorex," a woman asked, looking at me over lavender glasses.

"I didn't add to anything, if that's what you're asking."

"Mmmm!" they chorused.

They left after a host of suggestions, compliments and volunteering to model.

I found myself alone again. I began mixing paints.

Perfecting the pale pearl translucence of May's complexion took the rest of the morning. Satisfied with the blend finally, I dabbed the color onto her cheek. It came alive. Working slowly, I filled in the color on her sleek form.

A knock at the door pulled me away. I opened it to find a tall man with a shock of flowing white hair standing on the porch.

"I'm George."

"Come in George."

Thank god he had indeed put on pants and a shirt for the visit. He had to bend his neck to pass through the doorway.

"Is that it?" he asked, pointing to the painting.

"Yep."

"They're right, this is a masterpiece."

He moved closer. I thought to warn him about the wet paint, but he stopped.

"Teros said I would be taken by your work." George stared at the canvas. "I'm sure I've never seen anything quite so meaningful."

Odd word choice, but it sounded like a compliment.

"Thank you."

"No, I should be the one thanking you. I saw your face when you arrived a few days ago, and I would've bet my Kitchenaid you were done for. Looking at this, I know I would've lost." Tears formed in his gray eyes. He pulled off his glasses and wiped them away. "This gives me back my hope. Thank you."

I stared into his unusual face, unsure of what to say.

George looked at Danielle and May a moment longer before turning to the painting of Teros.

"You've caught his spirit here. That's not an easy thing to do," he said.

"Thank you."

"Dinner tonight should be pretty good."

"I'm looking forward to it, George."

He took a last look at the drawings of Teros I'd done on the first day and then left.

I painted until the gong sounded.

The dining room buzzed. It took me a while to realize they were talking about my paintings.

"You should do a showing here in the hall every couple of weeks while you're here," Priscilla said. "That way we can see your progress. After all that's why we're all here, to support each other," Priscilla said.

In the past I'd been reticent about showing my work before I thought it was   ready. Somehow this felt different. It felt okay, safe. Is this what my friend had meant about having her soul ripped away and replaced with something better?

"Sure, I'd love to get your input."

"I doubt if we can say anything that would make your work better my dear," the older woman from this morning said. "We just want to see it."

Several people agreed.

I hurried over to sit across from May and Danielle.

"Be sure to write down when and where you're showing. We're already making our own guest list," May said.

"And you don't have to worry about a bunch of freeloaders coming. We'll invite the folks we know who have some bucks," Danielle added.

Three monks, not including Teros, walked in from the kitchen carrying salad bowls. He must not be back yet. The door swung open again, and George came out wearing a white chef's uniform topped with a big white hat. The room went silent. Someone let out a small groan.

"Not the ten minute apology again. I thought we were over that," Henry whispered.

George shot him a look and then his gaze rested on me.

"The menu tonight is arugula salad ala George, rack of lamb with a basil mint sauce, potatoes with baby peas, and chocolate cake for desert. Bon appetite."

He spun on his heel and returned to his kitchen.

There was a pause before applause broke out.

"What did you say to George?" Henry asked.

"Nothing, he came over and looked at my work. He said he liked it."

"He must've more than just liked it. I can hardly wait to see your new stuff." Henry turned his attention to the salad set before him. He took a bite and rolled his eyes back in his head dramatically. "And, hallelujah, the food is still good!"

By the end of dinner, still no Teros, and my disappointment must've shown on my face.

"Hey, if the hard body doesn't show, our offer to take a walk on the softer side is still good." May said.

"I'm keeping it in mind, ladies." I said.

Outside, a monk or maybe another volunteer, approached. "Teros asked me to make sure you had everything you needed. I've drawn your bath and placed a snack in the refrigerator."

"Thank you?"

"I'm Brother John, like the song," he said, heading off any attempts at cleverness I might have considered.

"Thank you Brother John. Will he be back later tonight?"

"No, Teros volunteered to take care of some additional monastery business. He is one of our biggest supporters. He asked me to tell you he's sorry and remind you to concentrate on your work."

"So when is he expected back?"

"Not until Thursday."

"Damn it! Sorry Brother John"

Brother John raised his hand, dismissing my lapse of manners. His eyes were filled with concern.

Smiling I tried to suck it up for his sake, when all I really wanted was to go sit in a corner and wait for Teros.

"The chapel is open should you need to seek solace. It's over there."

He pointed to a grove of maples down the path from the hall.

"Thank you."

I couldn't possibly tell him the kind of solace I needed could not be found inside a place of religion.

"Can you do me a favor Brother John?"

I searched my pockets for the tiny pencil and sketch diary I always carried. After jotting my cell phone number on a page, I ripped it from the pad and passed it to him.

"If Teros calls again, will you give him my number?"

"Of course."

Brother John slipped the paper into the sleeve of his brown robe and glided away.

So, why didn't you just ask Brother John for Teros number? Simple, you don't want him to think you're some needy old broad chasing after a young piece of tail.

The bath only served to emphasize my loneliness and how much I missed sitting astride Teros' penis while being bathed by him. I climbed from the tub and toweled off. He'd been right about one thing. I did need to concentrate on painting. Although I seemed to have broken the block, I was not out of the woods yet. I had to produce a body of work for this show, not just a couple of good paintings.

It took an hour to decide that I couldn't possibly paint in my current mood. A walk might burn off some of the nervous energy tying my creative muscles and other things into knots.

Dressed in jeans, sweat shirt and tennis shoes, I jammed the little sketch diary and pencil in one pocket and grabbed Teros' flashlight. I hoped it would provide enough light for me to negotiate the path to the beach.

The circle of light played over the ground ahead of me as I walked the steep path. Midway, something scrambled through the underbrush startling me. The flashlight flew from my hand, bouncing away. It flickered and went out. Panic welled up as I pictured myself tumbling down the stair path and breaking a leg, or worse.

A moment passed before I realized a nearly full moon shined through the branches overhead. I could still see.

Walking past the spot where Teros' carving sat, I continued on to the fork I'd seen Henry and Priscilla follow earlier. As the path leveled out the soft liquid sound of water lapping the shore reached my ears and a stunning view of a moonlit cove showed through an opening.

Warm wind brushed through the trees carrying the scent of salt and evergreens. I breathed in deeply, savoring the incredible beauty of this setting. I pushed through the thickets, then froze at the sound of voices.

Henry and Priscilla walked nude from the water. Stopping, as if I'd asked them to pose, they folded together in an embrace.

Moonlight bathed their entwined bodies, hers light, his shadow. The waters of Puget Sound sparkled like shards of silver glass, licking gently at their ankles.

Candice Butler

Henry's dark form molded precisely against the curves of Priscilla's pale skin. Her breasts, small and loose with middle age, pressed the thick flesh and muscle of his mature chest. The composition they formed could not have been improved.

These were definitely not the sexy nubile bodies of young lovers. Instead their undeniable sensuality came from the very fact that they still believed themselves desirable enough to stand here, now, naked before each other.

Slowly Henry's head lowered and Priscilla's small face lifted to receive his lips. I swallowed against the lump in my throat.

Inspiration this perfect didn't happen often. And I knew better than to waste this one. I pulled the sketch diary and pencil from my pocket.

My mind and pencil freezing them in place, even after they moved further up the beach, like insects in amber. I sketched their beautifully imperfect bodies standing beneath the moon.

Last I got around to landscape; a tree limb filled the foreground, framing the couple in the distance. Bright bits flashed, catching the light as the dark water arranged and rearranged the shore. Gnarly stumps and twisted limbs decorated the ground surrounding a small crescent of sand. I drew in artist's shorthand, quick lines, a bit of shading. When I went to paint this, no more would be needed because nothing could wipe the splendor of this scene from my memory.

Unable to contain my excitement I scrambled back up the slope and raced to my cottage. May and Danielle's picture went over by the window next to Teros and a new canvas went up on the easel. Clipping the small sketch to the side and grabbing my pencil, I drew quickly, anxious to capture everything my mind and pencil had recorded.

I started out feeling like the picture would practically paint itself. By three o'clock reality kicked in. Why wasn't this working? I threw the charcoal pencil at the corner. My body screamed for food, rest, and Teros.

Brother John had left a turkey sandwich along with my desert in the refrigerator. I pulled them out and behind found a small bottle of amber colored wine.

Bless him, I could use a drink. I poured some of it into the glass and took a sip. A smoky sweetness danced over my tongue. Wow, delicious and it had a nice kick. I finished the glass and poured another before reading the handwritten label. *St. Catherine of Bologna Huckleberry Aperitif – Fall 2004.*

Starting in on the sandwich I walked back and forth in front of the drawing of Henry and Priscilla. Something was missing, but what? I tried adding more light, less light, reworking their expressions; his eyes, her lips.

I undressed for bed. As I stood before the full-length mirror, the last of the moon shown through the window. That's it! The picture wasn't missing anything, I'd added too much in the first place. I'd worked hours to perfect faces I hadn't been able to see in the moonlit darkness.

All of the yearning and desire I'd witnessed had not been in their expressions. It had manifested in the shapes of their bodies, the touching of their hands, the way they'd leaned toward each other, closing down the space between them when they joined; light and darkness, lines and shadows, positive and negative.

Now I knew what to do. No longer tired, I grabbed the paint pallet, squirted out a dollop of mars black and chromium white, a small amount of sepia and insubstantial hits of yellow, blue, and red and got down to work.

"Let's Get It On" rang out from my cell phone. It had been my son's idea of the perfect ringtone for his Motown-loving mother. I lay across the bed, naked and covered in paint. As I sat up to grab the phone, my work stared me in the face.

"Hello," I answered after the second chorus.

"Good morning, my darling Serena. Are you still in bed?"

My body snapped to attention at the sound of his voice.

I glanced down at my paint covered body.

"Kind of. How about you?"

"Yes, I'm staying in a suite at Tower A in a big, lonely bed."

"Pretty swanky for an art teacher," I said.

"A friend owns the building."

"You've got some swanky friends."

"Are you naked," Teros asked.

I chuckled. "Yes. Not that it's doing me any good."

"It can. Right now, you're lying under me and I'm sucking your breast. Close your eyes and imagine it."

I rolled over and did as he said, imagining the warm wetness of his mouth as he gently pulled my nipple between his lips.

"Mmm, and it feels wonderful," I said.

"Good girl, now I'm kissing my way down your luscious body and we both know where I'm going, so open for me. "

The scratch of his morning beard against the tender skin of my stomach caused me to squirm, but a strong hand steadied me. I jumped at the feel of his calloused fingertips sliding gently across the ridge of my clit. When my eyelids fluttered open for an instant, I thought I saw the dark top of Teros' head between my thighs.

"Uh uh, keep your eyes closed," he soothed through the telephone. "Mmm, I love your smell and your taste when you're all wet."

I groaned into the telephone as his tongue lapped my pussy. It all felt so real.

"Mmm," he said again. "I'm here to serve you Serena Davies, so tell me what you want."

"Keep doing what you're doing," I told him, panting into the telephone.

"As you wish," Teros said.

His tongue began a slow wet exploration, first licking, and then sucking the labia lips, before running the tip through the inner folds. Moaning softly, I writhed against the covers and stifled a scream, as his teeth raked against my newly sensitized clit.

His voice got huskier, "And did I ever tell you that you have the most exquisitely sensitive clit. All I have to do is give it a little lick, and your juices flood into my mouth." Teros' breathing grew heavy.

"Oh, my god Teros, what are you doing to me?"

"Shhh, tell me what you want, Serena."

He blew a warm breath over me amplifying my need until I thought I'd die from it.

"Please, please, please," I begged him.

"Please what Serena?" he asked, his voice full of humor.

"Please finish, please fuck me, please."

"As you wish."

The warm weight of his body pressed against mine. Then the smooth wet tip of his penis pressed into me, filling the empty, longing space.

As if it were all real, my body responded, closing around him as he entered me and welcomed him back, with heat and wetness. I smelled the aphrodisiac, rich male scent as he got close to climax and could feel his breath dance across my skin.

He was panting now.

"Come for me, Teros," I whispered into the telephone.

The slick sound of Teros stroking his cock reached me.

A guttural cry his body tightened against mine and felt the flood of the creamy stream of jism shooting into me. A scream of pure pleasure ripped from my lips.

Teros spoke first. "Serena, are you still there?"

I retrieved my cell phone from a fold in the quilt.

"Yeah, sorry, I didn't know you could do that to me without being here. You're fantastic."

"Hmm, you're not so bad at phone sex yourself.
"

"It felt like you were here with me."

"In every important way, I am," Teros said.

I couldn't stop my heart from doing a little happy dance.

"Brother John said you wouldn't be back on the island until Thursday."

"The monastery is having some financial problems. I'm trying to work a few things out for them."

"I miss – the real sex."

I mentally kicked myself, I started out to say I miss you, but I chickened out at the last minute.

"I miss you Serena, not just fucking you, but everything about you. How's the painting coming?"

"Pretty well, I've started a new work of Henry and Priscilla."

"I can hardly wait to see it, and you."

"Hurry back then." I said.

"I will."

"Okay."

He hung up first and suddenly I felt the giddiness of college days when I started dating someone new.

Teros misses me. Then fear doused my giddiness with ice water. At 58 years old, I shouldn't want or need to feel that way anymore.

After showering the paint off and dressing, I took one last look at Henry and Priscilla before dropping the cover over it.

Brother John waved me to a seat.

"I'll bring it. Coffee and oatmeal, right?"

I nodded. "Coffee mostly."

He shook his head. "Teros would never forgive me if I let you starve to death."

The dining room was deserted except for the two of us. Brother John set down the earthenware mug with the sugar and cream. "George insisted on making you some fresh oatmeal. It'll be few minutes."

"Thanks."

"You look tired. Did you work all night?"

"Practically, but it was good. This place has a remarkable affect."

"I'm glad. I passed your number on to Teros."

I felt myself blushing and hoped the brother didn't notice. "Thank you. He called me this morning."

"Good. Oh, I see George has put your bowl of oatmeal on the ledge." Brother John glided over and retrieved the oatmeal. How did he manage to do that?

"Anything else?" he asked after setting the bowl in front of me.

"No, thank you. Really, I'm sure you've got lots of more important things to do around the monastery. I'll manage until Teros gets back."

"Untrue. Ms. Davies, we believe the artists we nurture here are our most important job. So until Teros returns you are my most important job. I will be in the vegetable garden weeding should you need me."

"Then don't let me keep you Brother John and thank you again."

When I didn't show for lunch, Brother John deposited a tray on the porch. Grateful, I carried it in and devoured the chicken sandwich and fresh fruit salad. Searching through the stacks of stretched canvases, I located one of the small ones. I decided to paint a kind of a welcome home card for Teros, since I'd planned on something a bit more physical in celebration of his home coming.

Pulling the Greek god sketch I'd done of him, I taped it to the wall next to the window seat and stretched out with my paints. A peacefulness settled over me, as I sat working in that sunny window.

I looked at his face, squaring up the line of his jaw a bit more. Would a relationship even be possible outside of this idyllic setting?

A friend once told me that women like me in relationships like this are known as cougars. What a stupid, degrading nickname. It implied women are vicious predatory animals and reduced younger men to vulnerable not-too-bright prey. Nothing could be further from the truth between Teros and me. Not that it mattered, he hadn't given any indication he wanted anything beyond this three months.

He probably had friends, a life, maybe even a girlfriend somewhere that he would return to. I hadn't sought out this relationship, but I wasn't stupid enough to turn my back on it either. I'd treat it like summer camp, and at the end of this three months I'd pack up my paintings and go home.

"I might not get a happy ever after, but that doesn't stop me from having a happy right now," I said aloud.

The dinner gong rang, but I decided to keep working. I knew everyone would think I was brooding over Teros and they'd be right. Besides, I was also on a roll. I'd put the finishing touches on May and Danielle this afternoon. Henry and Priscilla's painting and the one of Teros, were also coming along nicely.

I'd never been able to work on this many pieces at one time. If I could maintain this pace, I'd have no problem having enough for the show.

I heard someone on the porch. Setting the pallet down, I opened the door. George stood outside with a loaded tray.

"You missed dinner. Everyone said you were probably working and Brother John said he'd bring you a sandwich, but I told him I'd bring you something."

"Come on in."

He moved past me and set the tray on the far end of the table.

"Is that your latest?" he asked, looking at the mostly black and white rendition of Henry and Priscilla.

"Yep."

He bobbed his head up and down.

"Mind if I look at it while you eat?"

I hadn't planned to stop, but the smells emanating from beneath the covered dishes started my mouth to watering.

"No, take your time," I said.

George pulled the covers off the plates, revealing a beautiful pork chop, whipped sweet potatoes, sautéed green beans and a slice of apple pie.

"It looks and smells delicious. Did you want to apologize first or can I start eating?"

George smiled and wandered over in front of the painting of Teros as a god. Focused on the painting of Teros, his face remained impassive, but I heard his sharp intake of breath. Then he moved to Henry and Priscilla. After a moment he pulled up the other chair and sat down in front of them.

I couldn't remember anyone ever giving my work such intense scrutiny. It felt unnerving.

"This one's even better than the others," he said quietly. "You seem to be drawing more deeply on your talent."

Okay, that remark hit the nail on the head.

"Thank you."

George twisted his head from side to side, up and down, as if he didn't want to miss one brushstroke. Finally he spoke again. "He doesn't see your imperfections. He's going to love you, you know."

I froze with the fork half way to my mouth. "What? Who?"

"Anteros. If he hasn't already, he's going to fall in love with you. That's what this painting is asking, and the answer is yes."

"It's actually Henry and Priscilla. I stumbled across them last night on the beach and they were so—" I choked up.

"They might be the subjects of the painting but they're not the question behind it. The answer is yes." George stood up and moved the chair back to the corner. "Just leave the tray on the porch. I'll see it gets picked up."

"George, am I that pathetically obvious?" I asked before he closed the door.

"No Serena, I think you're both just incredibly lucky."

Lying in bed I studied the painting of Henry and Priscilla. Had I really juxtaposed my own wishes and desires against their joyful moonlight tryst? After studying the painting I admitted George was absolutely right. So how accurate was his prediction about Teros? Those eyes of his saw a lot more than he let on.

I made sure my cell phone was within easy reach in case Teros called in the morning, and turned out the light.

Chapter Eight

All night I dreamed of sloping mountains, deep valleys, and tall trees. In that early morning state between waking and sleeping, I dreamed of Teros, his head looking up between the twin peaks of my thighs before he began to tongue my clit.

I awoke with a start. Oh my god, May had absolutely nailed it. Sex had been the driving force in a whole lot of my longing landscapes. Talk about your Freudian slips; for years I'd unknowingly substituted rolling hills for tight butts, giant trees for thick cocks, wide open valleys with meandering streams – enough! I got the point already!

I grabbed my sketch diary and pencil from the night table and laid out the idea for my next painting. I'd never accessed this many ideas or this much inspiration so quickly or so easily.

My stomach growled. Despite last night's fabulous supper, I was starving. I glanced at the time on my cell phone - a quarter to five. Breakfast usually didn't start until six, but George might be willing to slip me some coffee and a piece of his delicious crusty bread fresh from the oven. Donning jeans and a sweat shirt I hurried over to the great room.

The kitchen was empty. Outside in the courtyard behind the building, I could hear George singing, out by the massive wood-fired brick oven. A bright light poured through the stained glass back door. As I opened the door to the courtyard, waves of heat and light washed over me from the open oven.

George leaned into the crackling fire, retrieving loaves with his bare hands. I gasped. He spun around, orange flames dancing harmlessly over his skin.

Gold bands ringed his massive arms and a brown leather apron covered his otherwise nude body. Long silvery white hair flowed out behind him, dancing on the breeze. His entire body glowed from an inner light. His eyes, shimmering like polished silver disks, met mine.

"Serena!"

"George?"

"Stay down." A hand on my shoulder held me against the soft cushions of a sofa in the sharing area.

"I'm fine. What happened?"

George looked down at me with his normal gray eyes full of concern.

"I was carrying in bread from the ovens, when you came into the kitchen and fainted."

His eyes darted away for a second. "Did you work all night again?"

That's not how I remembered it. On second thought, I wasn't sure what I remembered.

"No, I had a great night's sleep and I'm not a fainter. When I saw you, you looked different, brighter, bigger. "

I shook my head from side to side, trying to hold onto the image, but it faded away fast like mist in sunlight.

"So was I better looking?" he asked, smiling.

"Well yeah, you were really hot with this buffed out body and really, really, great hair. I'd say gorgeous, god-like, even." I laughed.

He joined in. "Sounds like a great hallucination."

"I don't hallucinate either."

"So it's a morning of firsts." George looked away. "What brings you to my kitchen this early?"

"I'm famished and came over to hit you up for a cup of coffee. And a piece of that fresh bread I smell."

He let me up. "Come on in the back, I'll see what I can whip up."

The three-egg omelet flew four feet into the air, and executed a full somersault with a half twist before landing back in the skillet with a satisfying slap.

"Show off," I said.

George winked and slid his beautiful fluffy creation onto the plate in front of me.

"Eat up." He shoved a basket of fresh bread across the counter.

I dug into George's creation. "So do you know Teros well?"

"Yep, I've known Anteros since he was a boy. He was a serious kid even then, not at all like his brother."

"What did you mean when you said he would fall in love with me?"

"I was wrong."

My brain seized up, the right brain and left brain locked in battle. My intellect knew falling in love with Teros and having him love me meant nothing but trouble, but the artist couldn't think of anything I'd ever wanted so much.

"Oh, okay then. Could you pass the coffee?"

He picked up the pot and filled my cup.

George's expression softened. "I was wrong in saying that he would fall in love with you. He's already in love with you Serena."

Yes!

"So as an old friend of the family, should I be asking you what your intentions are?"

"Come on George, we're two old war horses who know how the world works." I said, pushing the last bites of omelet around on the plate. "I'd be the biggest liar in the world if I told you I didn't feel something for him, too. But we both know he's too young."

I wasn't ready to call what I felt for Teros love, yet every fiber in my being knew the truth.

George looked disappointed.

"He's a lot older in many ways than he looks." George said quietly. "But that shouldn't matter."

"It does matter."

"Tell me, what if I wanted to be with that lovely young poet or the equally beautiful erotic author? Would you automatically think there was something wrong with me?"

"No, I'd say you're a pretty typical male and then I'd remind you that they're both lesbians."

He shook his head sadly. "Not the point I'd hoped to make."

"You're a man, George. The rest of the world would call you a stud. It's different for women." I smiled. "I should've fallen for someone like you."

"And I wouldn't have objected to that, either," he said.

People started to filter into the dining room. "I should let you get back to work."

"Give both of you a chance, Serena. Anteros will surprise you, I promise."

"I'll think about it George. By the way, you make a killer omelet."

"That means a lot coming from a woman of your caliber."

My first serious art professor told me true artists use everything in their lives to make, or make better, their art. I agreed wholeheartedly, so I couldn't possibly let a perfectly good hallucination go to waste. Back in my cottage I sketched out my vision of George as god of the kitchen. Bulging arms, a barrel chest and behind that leather apron I'd glimpsed a golden girdle that barely shielded the bulge of his substantial genitals. I wondered what he'd think. Then I remembered he's a guy, he'd be flattered and probably ask why I hadn't made him bigger.

The noise from the engine of a small plane startled me away from my painting and brought a smile. Life here was so quiet I'd almost forgotten the usual din of mechanized life. Yet another reason it would be hard to leave when the time came.

My cottage door flew open, hitting the wall behind it. He stood there, big and gorgeous, a smile lighting up his face. Then he charged at me, lifting me from the chair and planting his lips against mine. I couldn't breathe, I didn't care. Our tongues did battle until we stopped, breathless.

"I couldn't wait to get back to you, so I forced them to wrap it up early and chartered a seaplane."

"God, I missed you too."

We tore at each other's clothes. Just outside the door, I heard an exclamation. Teros kicked it shut.

Pants still around my ankles, he yanked on a condom, pushed me down on the bed and shoved his penis home with a groan.

Clinging to each other we banged out all the frustration of being separated. I came first, with Teros quickly following me.

Lips plastered together, we stood beneath the warm shower.

"Did I hurt you?" Teros asked. "I tried to be gentle but I haven't been able to think of anything but fucking you since I left."

"You were pretty much all that I thought of, too."

He reached back, grabbing my butt, pulled against his erection and ground it against me until my knees went weak.

"Remember what I told you when I left, no painting and I'd cut you off?"

"Glad I painted then. And I'm anxious for you to see them. But not until you've taken care of a few things."

Teros eased down and blew a hot breath against my pussy.

"With pleasure."

The rest of the shower took a lot longer than it should have.

Teros stood behind me, his arms wrapped around my waist. A tremble went through him when I pulled the cover from the completed painting of Henry and Priscilla.

"It's wonderful," Teros whispered.

His arms tightened as I showed him the landscape interpretation of us in my sketch diary.

"So, what do you think?" I asked, half afraid he might not like something so intimate involving him.

His voice was low and full of emotion when he finally spoke. "It's amazing. I've always known you have a phenomenal talent, but these exceed everything I could've dreamed of for you."

Dreamed of for me. That zinger went straight to my heart. I loved him and there was no way around it. I pulled his lips down to meet mine. It had been a long time, if ever, that a man wanted something for me instead of from me.

I showed him the sketch of George.

"It's—" Teros paused. He looked upset.

"What? Don't you like it? Do you think George will be offended? You've got to admit, I did give him a great package and all."

"I'm certain he'll love it. They're all wonderful and you're wonderful and can we have a quickie now? Looking at your paintings makes me horny" Teros said pulling me against his ready cock.

A knock on the door interrupted what was shaping up to be a great fuck.

"Anteros, "Brother John called through the door. "Pardon me for disturbing you and Ms. Davies, but Brother Joshua is anxious to speak with you."

"Pleeese!"

I stuck my tongue into the tip of Teros' penis, giggling, as his voice went up two octaves.

"Bad girl," he growled quietly. "Please tell Brother Joshua I'll come to his office in a few minutes. Thank you, Brother John."

"I'll tell him. You're welcome."

Brother John hurried off the porch.

"Serena Davies that was totally uncalled for," Teros said sternly.

"So let me make it up to you." I took as much of that beautiful cock into my mouth as would fit, sliding my tongue along the sensitive vein and loving the sound of his groan. Teros reached down, grasping my head lightly between the palms of his hands. He moved his cock between my lips.

As the salty sweetness of his first cum touched my tongue, he froze and tried to pull out. I gripped his ass. I wanted to taste all of him. When he didn't continue, I slid the tip of one finger into his anus. He groaned. Another shudder passed through him, this time transmitting directly into my body. I felt it in my lips, a most delicious sensation.

"No, you mustn't "Teros said between clenched teeth.

I wriggled my finger into him past the first knuckle. He thrust his hips forward until his cock collided with the back of my throat. I loved giving head. But this was different. Sucking Teros cock was different. He tasted different too.

It didn't take long between fingering his anus and sucking his cock, before his breathing turned to panting. I felt his cock growing bigger inside my mouth. I continued gentle suction, playing my tongue around the pulsing head. I wanted, needed to taste him.

Suddenly hot come shot to the back of my throat, hot sweet, salty potent. The flood of jism sparkled across my tongue with the effervescent sparkle of good champagne. Hungrily, I swallowed the flow. Stars exploded behind my eyes, and around me the room exploded with lights and colors like the fourth of July.

Wow, had someone put LSD in the orange juice this morning? Teros' magnificent body appeared to glow with golden light as he released the last of his seed.

My body poised on the knife edge of a powerful orgasm. Colors continued to dance off the walls and the room spun like a top. The climax hit me. Lightheaded my body lifted above the earth. A second climax followed on the heels of the first. I collapsed. Teros picked me up from the floor and carried me to the bed.

Suffocating and drowning at the same time, I couldn't catch my breath. Murmuring my name, Teros smoothed my hair from my eyes.

"What's happening?" I managed to ask through the riot going on inside my head.

"I love you," Teros said, burying his tongue inside me.

I arched against his mouth.

"Too much." I tried to twist away from him.

"Let me, you need this," he murmured.

A tidal wave of emotion washed over me.

"Teros," I said. Then like a drowning swimmer I went under again. "Help me."

Teros' green eyes filled with worry. "Shhh," he said slipping two fingers into my pussy. Desperate to reach a climax my body writhed in anguish.

"Fuck me please," I begged. I grabbed for his cock. Tears rolled down my cheeks. "Please fuck me Teros. Make it stop."

I came again, this time bigger than the last, but the need only grew stronger. The sound of roaring waves filled my head. I knew the sound was my own pulse.

"I'm so sorry. You'll be okay baby. I'm with you Serena."

Teros' hands steadied me. He covered my mouth with his. He pulled my tongue into the warmth of his mouth, his gentle suction seemed siphoned off the desire. Slowly, the frantic need dulled. The feeling of urgency subsided.

Before I dropped into sleep I heard him whispering, "I forgot how fragile you are. Forgive me. I love you Serena."

Teros sat on the side of my bed in his utility kilt, the bag of carving tools by the door.

"What time is it?"

"Seven a.m. Hurry up, sleepy head. I want to work on your bust."

"Oh god, don't tell me I fell asleep during sex again."

He clucked his tongue. "Second time, I might get a complex or something."

Panic gripped me, then vanished.

"Did we actually fuck?"

"Oh, yeah, a few times," Teros said. "Now I'm really getting an inferiority complex."

He seemed to be watching me carefully.

Something didn't feel right, as if I'd lost a chunk of time.

"So hurry while the light's still good."

"How about talking to Brother Joshua?" I asked.

"Talked to him while you were sleeping," he said. "It's warm outside, I thought we'd swim a little afterwards."

"Should I bring a suit?

Teros waggled his eyebrows. "I don't think you'll need one."

Chapter Nine

My life on the island settled into a blissful routine of waking up and being fucked by Teros, painting, until lunch, and fucking Teros, long walks around the island, more painting, dinner, sharing the work of some of the most talented, generous people I'd ever met in my life, and spending my nights, fucking and unfortunately falling more deeply in love with Teros.

At the end of the second month I took the earlier suggestion and brought over eight paintings in various stages of completion to present to the group. These included the one of Henry and Priscilla that I hadn't had the courage to show until now, and George's hallucination portrait. Teros and George helped me arrange them around the sharing area.

"It's stunning," Priscilla said, viewing the picture of her and Henry.

"Brilliant the way you used black and white to make both literal and subjective statements. You're one hell of an artist," Henry said.

I pulled them away from the group.

"I'm really sorry. It was an accident that I came across you at the beach. I didn't stick around, but the moonlight, the beach, you two together. I really couldn't help myself. It demanded to be painted. But I don't have to show it publicly if you'd rather I didn't."

"We're really quite flattered," Priscilla said. "You made us look beautiful. Besides, I'd already said I would love to model for you."

"Are you kidding, you've got to include it in your show and we'll be there," Henry said.

The unfinished painting of George as the sensual god of the kitchen, made the biggest hit.

"It's hard to believe our George is hiding all that hotness behind that apron," said Madeline Barton, a middle-aged writer of speculative science fiction.

"Excuse me, did you say hotness?" I asked her.

"Yes, I said hotness." She looked at me over the rim of her lavender glasses. "Just because I have grown kids doesn't mean I don't keep up. And I'll definitely be spending more time in the kitchen." Her laughter rang out and I found myself joining her.

Eventually George threatened to throw dinner out if we didn't all sit down and eat.

May and Danielle gushed over the finished painting of them. Danielle handed me a piece of paper. "Here's our telephone numbers and email addresses. Please, please let us know the date of your opening. We want to be there," she said.

"You did us proud," May said with sudden tears in her eyes.

I wrapped an arm over her shoulder. "What's wrong?"

"It's nothing, really. I'm the emotional one and we're leaving tomorrow."

"Oh." While I'd always known people would be coming and going, including me, May's announcement weighed on me like a lead blanket. Partly because I would miss both of them, but mostly because it reminded me I'd be leaving soon, too. Damn it all! How had I allowed myself to become so dependent on Teros, so connected and caught up in whatever this thing was between us?

"Well then, we need to celebrate," I said with false gaiety.

Table talk and wine flowed freely. George even sent out a special Port made at the monastery for the sharing of Danielle's completed poem and the final chapter of May's erotic mystery.

May's talent was unmistakable and despite her unvarnished descriptions of every sexual proclivity I'd ever heard of and a few I hadn't. I, along with everyone else got caught up as much in the in whodunit part of the story as who would fuck who next.

Raucous applause broke out as her sexy heroine, Inspector Dennison, who had a penchant for riding crops and red lace lingerie, peeled away the layers of deception and articles of clothing to reveal the killer.

I couldn't be sure if it was way too much wine or the fabulous fucking by proxy that May had treated us to, but by the time Teros and I made it back to my cottage I wanted him more than ever.

"I'm going to miss them," he said pulling my shirt over my head. He grasped my tits and squeezed the nipples.

Suddenly the fear and frustration, I'd been holding at bay, exploded into anger; anger at him, at myself, at the whole damned world that said this relationship had to end here.

Leaving Teros would rip my heart out. Why had I allowed this to happen? At my age, I damn well knew better.

After he finished undressing me, I practically tore that brown robe from Teros' body. I leaned over the table, resting my breasts against the cool wood.

Teros tried to pull me around to kiss me. But I couldn't bear to see his face, or look into his eyes knowing it would soon be over for us.

"No, damn it!" I screamed. "I want you to fuck me from behind. Hard."

"What's wrong, Serena?"

Grief rolled over me in waves so potent, I felt myself gagging on it. Teros' arms circled my waist and he rained kisses onto my back.

"Tell me what's wrong," he said.

"You said you were here to serve me, right?" I said through clenched teeth. Tears burned down my cheeks.

"Yes, of course." Concern colored his voice.

"Then fuck me hard. And if you can't I'll go find someone who can and will."

I listened as he stretched the condom on. His hands gripped my hips with bruising force. I didn't care. I savored the pain.

Teros rammed his full length into me, with one brutal stroke. Pulling out he rammed into me again, slamming his balls against my butt, smashing my breasts into the table top. Relentlessly, he drove his cock into me.

"Is this what you wanted?" he asked after a moment, and then jammed himself in so hard it knocked the breath from me. "You want to feel pain, so you don't have to feel love?" His cock slammed home again. "I love you whether you want me to or not. He grunted pulled back. "And I won't leave you Serena." He grunted again.

He grew bigger inside me until it felt like his cock would split me wide open. I wanted the physical pain and the angry lust to be the only things I felt. He shoved his cock in deeper. I tried in vain to convince myself he was just a good fuck, and I didn't feel anything else for him. I didn't want him in my life forever. When I left this island paradise I would find someone else who could take his place.

Lies, all of it. But I desperately wanted, needed to believe them.

As he pounded into me, passion laced with despair drove me toward orgasm. Now angry too, Teros rammed his cock into me like a piston. His hot breath blew across my back and his balls beat bruises into my backside.

"Ohhh!" The orgasm overwhelmed me. Biting into the flesh of my forearm I screamed out my pain and frustration.

Almost before he'd finished coming, Teros yanked himself out. He went into the bathroom. I heard the shower come on briefly. Then he came out.

"I know what you're feeling. I understand that you'd rather hurt than love me, and that's your choice to make. But don't ever ask me to do that to either of us again." Teros threw on his robe and left.

I ignored the impulse to run after him or throw myself face down on the bed and bawl like a melodramatic teenager.

Instead I sat in the window seat staring over the tree tops at the waves. I'd started down this road knowing the exact date it would end. Teros had a right to be angry with me. Punishing him for the way of the world had been mean and unfair.

As the sun came up I realized how incredibly lucky I'd been to have him even for three months. So I went to tell him that.

Before I could muster the words of my apology, Teros wrapped his strong arms around me, covered my lips with his and he kissed me breathless.

"You're forgiven," he said.

Chapter Ten

Only fourteen days remained to my stay. The realization hung over my head like the Sword of Damocles. Brother Joshua might let me extend it another week, if there were room, I thought with hope. What would be the point? My gallery opening, the reason I'd come here in the first place, was in three weeks. I had to go.

When Teros and I were together I studiously avoided all talk about what might happen next. I couldn't wouldn't subject either of us- okay me, to the ridicule of some desperate May-December love affair. The real world would not be kind or forgiving and it could ruin both of our careers, not to mention our lives. I'd always hated The Graduate movie and I wouldn't become another Mrs. Robinson.

Unable to sleep, I painted until the sun came up. Tired, I glanced at the bed where Teros and I had spent so many erotic and tender hours, and cursed it. He'd wanted to spend the night with me last night, but I'd begged off, saying I needed to work.

After taking a shower, I dressed in sweatshirt and jeans, making sure to grab a belt. All the clothes I'd brought fell off my new, trimmer figure.

I loaded my sketch diary, a bottle of water and a bag of George's granola in a small pack.

Heading in the direction of the rising sun, I decided to walk around the small island counter clockwise. That way the steepest parts came first and I would be rewarded at the end with the beautiful glen and its moss draped waterfall.

I really had no choice. The sooner I weaned myself off this relationship with Teros, the better it would be for both of us.

I scrambled up the steep hillside. From the beginning I'd told myself the shiny newness of fucking him would wear off after a couple of dozen times and I kept up the lie even when I knew the truth. It hadn't. Instead my desire for him grew stronger, and morphed into something deeper, almost without notice. Looking back I couldn't say when I'd come to feel just being with him was as good as fucking him. Maybe that had been the case from the moment I stepped off that boat.

At the top of the hill I took a seat on a rock and looked out over the stunning panorama. In the distance some of the closer islands arched emerald green from the blue water. The smell of pines and cedars filled the air. This beautiful setting should have brought me peace. Unfortunately I felt anything but.

From here the path dropped steeply until I could no longer walk. My feet slipped on loose stones and I fell, sliding down the path on my butt.

The hopeless romantic in me asked, "What if you could have a relationship with Teros off the island? Of course you can't. You don't even know if he lives in Washington. And you didn't ask him because you didn't want to be tempted," practical me responded.

Sliding to a stop midway along the path, I sat breathing hard and listening to the sound of dirt and rocks rolling off the cliff. After a long drink from the water bottle, I changed course, taking the easier walk down to the water's edge.

The path came to an abrupt end and I dropped a short distance into the water. Even in summer the ice cold water cramped my toes as I splashed through the shallows around deadfalls.

At Henry and Priscilla's beach, a band tightened around my heart. I hurried past it. They could share the life together I couldn't have with Teros.

Thankfully the climb to the waterfall was brief but incredibly steep from this direction. It left no room for thoughts beyond finding the next hand hold or ledge to step up on and grabbing for small saplings clinging to the rocks.

Near the top, firs shared the space with broad leaf maples turning a ruddy golden color. A thick stand of Douglas fir guarded the entrance to the falls. I began pushing through them, but stopped at the peal of a woman's laughter.

Should I make some sort of noise to announce myself? Especially since I'd already gained the reputation as the group voyeur? Too bad this was the only path forward and I didn't have the energy to return to the monastery the strenuous way I'd come. I guess I could wait, or maybe they were only swimming in the blue-green pool beneath the falls.

I hesitated before peeking through the foliage. The sight of two of them caused my breath to catch in my throat.

George stood beneath the ice cold stream, nude, his massive legs astride two boulders, and the long tapered legs of a woman circled his waist. Her slender arms draped his broad shoulders. His long silvery white hair trembled each time he drove himself into her. Unadulterated lust, like a warm wind blew around them, smelling like roses and feeling like the air right before a lightning strike.

Mesmerized, I watched them fuck. My own body responded to every masterful stroke with desire and envy.

The woman gasped a musical sound that got higher each time George drove into her. For an old guy I had to admire his stamina as he pumped his hips between her exquisite legs, stroke after stroke. She came with the vibrato of a coloratura soprano hitting the perfect high C. George moaned and then bellowed as he climaxed. The sound drowned out the roar of the falls.

After kissing her, George lowered the woman to the ground as if she were made of fine china. One look at her ethereally, delicate beauty and I believed she might actually be.

Naked, she was perfect, her olive gold skin flawless and sumptuous figure, full breasts with perfect rose colored nipples that spit in the eyes of gravity, a butt rounded like a melon, wide flaring hips, a tiny waist and long legs. Surprised by the arousal she awakened in me, I found myself staring in awe at her the large pink clit parting the hair of her mound and wondering if it could possibly taste as good as it looked. I tried to look away from her and when that didn't work I forced my eyes to examine the rest of the woman.

Her hair shined blue-black in a ray of light penetrating the trees and hung in long waves below her waist. Full rose colored lips smiled, and her green eyes danced with laughter. There were no words, even for an artist that could describe her incredible beauty. She could have been a goddess, if such beings existed.

Where had she come from?

Then it hit me. I was looking at Teros' Aphrodite in the flesh. I ignored the pang of jealousy, although her unparalleled splendor could make any woman jealous.

She shook her head, sending a shower of water over George who laughed like a man much younger than his apparent age.

He turned around to retrieve his towel. A tiny gasp escaped me. No golden girdle surrounded his loins, but the bakery god painting did George no favors. Despite the cold water his thick cock still hung over his thigh. And from the driving strokes I'd witnessed, he more than knew how to use it.

"Serena," George's voice called out to me, as he wrapped a towel around his waist.

Heat rose to my face as I stepped from the bushes into the small clearing. The woman slowly tied blue pareo around her curvaceous figure.

"I didn't mean to intrude," I said, still unsure how he'd known I was there.

"Not to worry," the woman said. Her voice had a deep sexiness to it that suited the rest of her.

Heat washed through me.

"We knew you would be coming this way. So we decided to amuse ourselves until you got here." She smiled at George and I watched the towel rise in front.

"Serena, this is Anteros' mother, A—"

"Agnes," she said interrupting him.

I should've guessed. She had the same deep peridot green eyes as her son.

"It's nice to meet you Agnes." I extended my hand and she took it in an elegant, cool grip.

I'd run across some inappropriately named people in my life, but this woman was definitely no Agnes.

"Teros talks about you constantly. He's in love with you, you know," Agnes said casually.

So much for the small talk.

"And that doesn't bother you?"

"Not in the least. I'd be worried for you if it were his brother. But Anteros does not give his love often or easily and when he does there's nothing on this earth to match it. So if that is something you want, you should think long and hard before discarding it."

"Agnes, let's be frank, shall we? You and I look to be close in age, which makes me old enough to be Teros' mother."

Her laughter startled me and went on forever, stopping only when George gave her a stern look.

"But you're not his mother Serena." She hiccupped down another laugh. "I'm sorry. I didn't mean to make light of your concern for the wellbeing of my son. It's obvious to me that you love him also. But he's past the age where I question why or who he chooses to love."

That's very understanding of you.

"I'm sure you're the same with your own son. Why do you think your age should concern me anyway?"

How had she known I had a son? That thought was followed immediately by why in the world am I arguing with her?

"Let's just say I'm well past the stage of producing grandchildren, for one thing." I reminded her.

Agnes laughed so hard this time George stepped closer and shook her lightly.

"Be nice Agnes," he admonished.

"I really am sorry, Serena. Believe me my other son has made sure that I've got plenty of grandchildren."

Agnes shook her heard. The long hair swayed seductively side-to-side, still moving after she stood perfectly still, almost as if it had a mind of its own.

"Your life is so fleeting. I don't understand how you could deny something so precious and as rare as love." Her beautiful face grew sad for a moment. Then she turned a startlingly erotic gaze on George.

"Let me tell you something it's taken me a very long time to learn, Serena. Love almost never comes in the vessel we expect or believe it should come in."

She smiled at George, who swelled up, in more ways than one under her alluring gaze.

"The wise woman will look past the vessel to enjoy the special wine inside."

The lusty looks passing between George and Agnes should've boiled the water fall. His towel fell to the rocks.

Okay, time for me to go.

"I'll consider that." I said, picking up my pack and hurrying to the other end of the path.

"I truly hope you do. If it's my blessing you need, then you have it." Agnes said, already stripping off the pareo.

I hurried up the slope until I was well out of sight and earshot. Sitting down next to the stream that fed the fall I tried to not think about what the mother of my lover and George were doing at this moment.

Pulling out my sketch diary and pencil I began drawing. By keeping my hands moving I could sort through my feelings. What if Agnes was right, should I be thinking twice before deciding I had no future with Teros?

A sound of breaking branches and footsteps caused me to look up. Teros approached on the path from the monastery.

He smiled, sending a flash of heat through me.

"I'm sorry about last night," I said.

"I do understand. Loving you has consumed me to the point where I can't contemplate losing you either. That's why I think we should talk about something more long term."

"Hey, how did you know I was here?" I asked, quickly changing the subject.

"I always know where you are," he said simply.

Had he meant that in a figurative way? I opened my mouth to ask, but when my eyes met that steady green stare and the passion burning behind it, the question disappeared from my mind.

"I met your mother. She was with George at the falls.

"My mother?" Teros' look turned worried.

"Agnes. A strikingly beautiful woman, a lot like her son."

He kissed me for that.

"What did my parents have to say?"

"Okay, that's news. Are you saying George is your father?"

"Stepfather, actually, but he was a lot more attentive than my real father."

"Agnes really didn't seem to mind I was sleeping with you."

"Probably because she knows sleeping is not what we're doing." Teros smiled.

"I mean I'd have expected your mother to be a bit more upset about the difference in our ages."

That worried look passed over his face again.

"So what did she say, exactly?"

"Well, when I told her she couldn't expect any grandchildren she laughed so hard George had to shake her. Then she said she had plenty. She also told me you were worth hanging on to."

He seemed to relax. "Did she convince you, or do I need to go commit matricide?"

"I'm not convinced that we can make this thing between us work, but I've decided to take your mother's advice, at least while I'm here."

"I want more. You know that, but I won't press you for an answer right now."

Teros lips covered mine, his tongue slipping between my teeth. I reached through the opening in the thick material of the monk's robe, knowing he'd be erect and ready for me.

Teros groaned, pulling away. "Sorry, I promised Brother John I'd help get Maplewood and Spruce ready for the two artists coming in tomorrow."

My disappointment must have shown on my face. He kissed the frown lines from my forehead. "I guess we'll have to make it a quickie then," he murmured jerking down the zipper on my jeans.

Watching George and Agnes go at it had me readier than I'd thought. Teros slid the jeans down my hips and pulled a condom from his pocket before lifting the robe. As usual he was wonderfully naked.

Really much easier, I wondered if those robes came in my size, until he shoved his cock into me. Then my only thought was how I could possibly live without this, without him.

Two weeks flew by as I knew it would. My last day, I finished packing up after breakfast. Teros and I hadn't made any firm plans except he'd come to stay with me for a week or two after he finished his quarter of teaching. We would play it by ear from there.

I took a last look around the cabin to make sure I wasn't forgetting anything. Time to reenter the real world. I pulled out my cell phone and turned it back on. It beeped almost immediately showing I had a message. I punched the voice mail button in the speed dial.

"Hey Mom, I knew you didn't want to be bothered while you were working, so I waited until your last day. I'm planning to come up for your big show. Hope the retreat did you some good. Call me when you get back to Seattle. Oh yeah, if you get a chance, tell Teros to give me a call. The Greek Consulate here bought his Aphrodite from the pictures he sent. His art department is going to make a killing. I love you, Mom."

The voice mail message ended. I stared at the cell phone in my hand, tempted to replay my son's message again. But I didn't need to.

Teros and my son Max were colleagues, friends. Why in hell hadn't Teros told me?

And here's to you Mrs. Robinson, Heaven holds a place for those who pray, hey, hey, hey.

"I loaded the rest of your things onto the boat." Teros stopped in the doorway.

"You should've told me you work with Max," I said to him.

His green eyes met mine. "I'd planned to, but I knew it would drive you away from me."

"You were right. I don't know why I thought I could do this."

I walked over to bed to collect my bag. I could feel his eyes on my back.

"Please Serena think about what you're doing. I love you." Teros said quietly.

"I love you too. But I can't."

"Why? Why should we be concerned what people say or think? Damn it Serena, don't you even care enough to try?"

He came up behind me, and wrapped his arms his arms around my waist. I melted against him.

"It would destroy me."

I knew this was a lame-assed, chicken excuse, but it was also true. Unfortunately I'd gotten too old and too tired not to care what people said and thought anymore. Rebellion is for the young. I craved a sense of peace in my life.

"I can't convince you?" he asked.

I shook my head.

Teros' lips covered mine and our tongues entwined for the last time. Beneath the soft fabric of his monk's robe, I felt his hard body and took a long slow inhale, savoring this last smell of him. My mouth treasured his taste, every cell of my body responded to the need in him. I wanted to remember it all because I wasn't fool enough to think I'd ever find any of this with anyone again.

Chapter Eleven

Sophia Reynolds circled through my dining room for the third time. Her stilettos making tiny marks in the hundred year old original maple floor while the glass of wine in her hand remained untasted.

She stopped at each painting, examining them as if she couldn't believe her own eyes. Sophia had been here for almost half an hour and she still hadn't said a word.

I should've been nervous since right now, my career hung in the balance, but I didn't need Sophia Reynolds or anyone else to tell me these paintings represented the best work I'd done in my entire life. If she chose not to show them in her gallery, finding another wouldn't be a problem.

I sipped cool Pinot Grigio from my own glass and waited.

"I'm completely blown away!" she said finally. "My god, Serena, I really didn't think you had this, these, in you."

"Thank you."

Sophia took a sip from the glass. "They're fabulous. People are going to go completely mad for them and for you. I just wish you had more."

"I did all of these in three months. That's faster than I've ever painted in my life."

"No, don't get me wrong. I wasn't trying to disparage your efforts. Oh my god, how could I? Every last one of them is spectacular. Michael predicted you were on the verge of breaking out. He had been tracking your work for years. But I doubt if even he saw this coming."

I felt myself cringe at her mention of Michael. Despite being innocent, mostly anyway, I still felt guilty about being the other woman. How did one apologize for that sort of thing?

"When will he be over to see them?" I asked. Truth be told, I never wanted to see Michael Reynolds again, especially not in my home.

"Michael won't be coming." Sophia's voice dripped with contempt. "We're getting a divorce. Didn't you read about it in the paper?"

"I'm sorry, I didn't know. No newspapers, radio, or television at St. Catherine's," I said.

"Sounds like heaven. Anyway since my money bought the gallery, I'm keeping it."

Embarrassed, I met her steady gaze. "You know, I really believed him when he said that you and he had separated."

Sophia's brittle laugh rang out. "Michael is very good at a lot of things, particularly cheating and lying. You were not the first, Serena, or the last, or even the only one at the time."

Touché, now I feel much better.

Her hand shook as she lifted the wine glass to her bright red lips. "I finally got tired of our little arrangement, and tired of him." She took another sip. "He's a lousy husband, but he could spot talent. And he certainly hit it out of the park with you."

I didn't want to talk about Michael Reynolds anymore. After Teros, it seemed impossible that I could have mistaken anything I felt for Michael as love or even affection.

"When do you want to do you the installation? I have some definite ideas on how the paintings should be sequenced in the space," I asked, anxious to talk about something else.

"I thought we could meet with the lighting designer and painter on Sunday. Then they could complete their work by Tuesday and we could start hanging on Wednesday. "

"That's cutting it kind of close."

"I agree, but I don't want anyone getting sneak peeks. This show is going to go nuclear. Don't worry we'll be ready for the art walk on Thursday. I'll bring in some extra help if we need to. We're going all out on this showing. I can hardly wait," Sophia said.

"Sounds good."

She watched me over the rim of her glass.

"Do you mind if I say something that's not too nice?"

"I fucked your husband, so I guess you're entitled to a free shot." I said, bracing myself for whatever came next.

She laughed. "Believe me when I say I'm over that. Although one day I may ask you to share that technique you were using when I walked in on you two. Michael actually raved about it."

Heat flooded my face.

Sophia noticed. "It's over, really. But, while these paintings are totally fabulous, you'll excuse me if I say you look like hell."

Until today I hadn't gotten out of my bathrobe. I looked down at the baggy cropped pants and shirt I thrown on for her visit. Between the great sex, great food, and daily walks, and because I'd never owned a scale I couldn't be sure how much weight I'd lost. Nothing seemed to fit anymore.

"I dropped a few pounds and I've been meaning to go shopping since I got back. I just haven't gotten to it yet."

Sophia looked skeptical. "A few pounds? You've lost half a person at least and you're depressed, Serena. Depression hangs off you worse than that horrendous outfit."

I thought about denying it, but why bother?

"Please don't tell me any of this," she waved a manicured hand at my body, "is due to Michael. Because trust me; he's so not worth it."

"Michael doesn't have anything to do with it."

"Glad to hear that. Now, I hope you won't fight me on this. We need to create a whole new Serena Davies for this show."

I shrugged, not really caring what she did; what anyone did for that matter.

She pulled out her cell phone and punched in a number.

"Hello this is Sophia Reynolds. Does Marlo have an opening for a very important friend of mine? Yes, Tuesday would be perfect and a week from Thursday afternoon, she'll come in with me. Perfect." Sophia looked over at me and smiled. "Her name is Serena Davies. She needs color, a trim, blow out, the works along with a manicure, pedicure and make-up. Great and put it on my account. Thank you."

"Sophia, I really don't think—"

"Serena if it's the money, don't worry. We're both going to make a killing with these paintings. And when you're feeling bad, I've always found pampering yourself to be the best medicine." Sophia punched some more numbers into her phone. "I'm also calling my personal shopper at Nordstrom to make an appointment for you."

I opened my mouth to protest.

Sophia shushed me. "I don't want to hear it. That earth mother garb may have been just the thing for your landscapes. I actually thought it kind of worked. But now, different paintings, a more sophisticated feel, and you need a different look. Agreed?"

Relieved when Sophia finally left, I returned to my studio. Now that my artistic block had been removed, I couldn't seem to stop painting, regardless of the emotional turmoil. Worse, no matter how hard I tried to push Teros away, the closer he hovered in my thoughts.

Someone had once told me the difference between artists and regular people is that artists use their pain to create, rather than whining about it. I stood in front of my easel, letting that pain guide my hand.

A family portrait of mother and son began to take shape; black hair, green eyes, golden-olive skin, and the unrelenting sexuality that poured off both of them and laid siege to everyone in its path.

Seeing Agnes at the falls with George, I'd known I wasn't the only person totally consumed by the magnetism both mother and son wielded. George's face held that same look of joy, yearning and utter wonder that I felt whenever Teros and I made love.

Could I paint them so other people could experience even a hint of their power? I had to try.

My cell phone rang. I set the brush down. .

"Hello."

"Hi Mom, you didn't call me back." Max sounded worried. I probably should have called him, but what would I have said? Hey, son, how are you doing? Good, by the way I'm fucking one of your friends?

"Max. I'm sorry, I meant to."

"I talked to Teros."

My heart sped up. "He's there?"

"Yeah, I picked him up from the airport last night," Max said.

"Did he say anything?"

"He told me he's in love with you."

A tear rolled down my cheek, followed by another and then another. Despite Max being a well respected psychologist, this wasn't the kind of conversation I'd ever expected to have with my son.

"He's a great guy Mom. It really would not bother me in the least if you ended up together."

"Glad to hear I have your approval. But I don't need it you know, since I'm the mother and all."

"Sarcasm is a defense mechanism. Remember, I know you and I know when you're hurting." Max let out an exasperated sigh. "All I'm saying is he loves you. So, he's younger. So what? He loves you."

I tried to speak. Sniffed, and tried again.

"Did I mention how much I love you," I said.

"All the time and avoidance is another defense mechanism. We'll talk when I get there. Don't worry about picking me up at the airport, I'm renting a car."

"I'll clean out your room."

"See you soon Mom. You deserve to be happy, really."

I clicked off the telephone, feeling worse, if possible. It rang again, startling me.

"Forget something Max?"

"Not Max, but how is he doing these days?"

"Nola! Tell me you're coming to my show on Thursday. I really could use a friendly face."

"Of course I'll be there. I put it on my calendar months ago." Nola paused. "Are you okay, you don't sound good?"

"I'm fine. I've been painting a lot, so I'm a little tired. I'll tell you about it later. Have you finished moving?"

"Sort of, I'm one of the newest owners at Tower A. You've gotta see this place," Nola said.

"I can't wait, but I'm tied up until after the opening."

"No hurry. I'm still buried in boxes. Are you sure there's nothing I can do?"

"Not yet. I'll let you know."

Nola and I had been propping each other up through break-ups since our days as undergrads at the 'U,' actually she did most of the propping. Later, I'd let Nola shower me with sympathy coupled with judicious amounts of practicality.

That steady-feet-on-the-ground engineer-minded sensibility would remind me 58-year-old women should have gotten past this falling in love crap, especially with thirty-something men. Right now I just wanted to wallow.

"Okay, I'll see you next Thursday then," Nola said.

I hated being the source of that worry in her voice, but it couldn't be helped. "We'll talk. I promise."

Between the installation and Sophia's extreme make over efforts, I barely had time to breathe, let alone brood. Still, I fell into bed each night trying desperately not to think about Teros and failing miserably.

I'd decided early on that these paintings should be hung in the order I'd created them. Tears burned at the back of my eyes as we hung the painting of Teros. Sophia noticed.

"Exquisite. Is he the one?" she asked, passing me a glass of champagne. Sophia used champagne to lubricate everything. Right now, it didn't seem like such a bad plan. I accepted the tall flute and took a sip.

"I despise that prejudice against older women with younger men, which is so not the case when the roles are reversed" She sipped her champagne.

I nodded.

"I think it's about time that smart women like us, said fuck that shit," Sophia said.

Upon hearing this street-tough profanity coming from the lips of the prim old-moneyed Sophia Brookshire Reynolds, champagne blew out my nose.

"Okay Sophia, don't hold back or anything on my account."

"No really, I'm tired of it. That song had it completely right. Age ain't nothin' but a number."

"What happened? Did you start subscribing to the R & B oldies channel on HD radio?"

She laughed. "It's one of my favorites. Do you remember that computer security CEO I told you about?

"The twenty-seven year old?"

"He's twenty-nine and I'm only 42. He keeps asking me out. And unlike Michael I don't have to worry about him being interested in my money. He's one of richest men in this city. I think I'm going to say yes."

My painting of Teros and Agnes was coming out better than I hoped.

After several minutes of gasping, Sophia said, "We've got to include it in the show."

"It's not quite finished."

"No one will know that except you. My god, no wonder you fell so hard. I'm heading back to the gallery and rearrange everything to make room. You put whatever finishing touches on it you need to for now. Trust me; we've got to include this painting. "

It was well after midnight by the time I got home to find a dozen perfect red roses on my porch.

The card read, "I know you'll do well tomorrow night, because you have a remarkable talent. Love, Teros."

The deep yearning I'd tried hard to ignore the pain that slashed through me as I re-read his card. Thank god none of my neighbors were still up to witness me completely breaking down on my front porch.

Tears poured down my face as I collapsed into a sobbing heap. I don't know how much time passed before I finally stood up, hugging the flowers to my chest and went inside.

As I climbed into bed I took one last look at the vase of roses and heard that old saying; "the heart wants what the heart wants," repeating itself in my head.

Max arrived mid-morning Thursday, pulling up into the driveway in a silver Mustang convertible. Just seeing him made tears well up in my eyes. When had I gotten to be so emotional?

"How are you doing Mom?" Max asked.

"I'm fine, really."

"Liar. I had a beer with Teros last night and if it's any consolation he also looks like a train wreck."

"A train wreck! I lost a lot of weight, and I'm healthier than I've been in decades. How can I look terrible?"

Max laughed. "You look great Mom, on the outside. Why don't you call him?"

"Why don't you mind your own bees wax?"

"Nice try Mom, but I'm past the age where you can hide things from me. I'm also too old to be shocked that my mother engages in sex."

"How about being shocked because your mother has sex with your friends?" I wished I could recall the words as soon as they came out of my mouth.

Max's expression did not change.

"Forget it. I don't want to talk about this now. Your room's made up and I've got an appointment at the salon. Must look good for tonight."

I left Max in the living room, shaking his head.

Nordstrom's had completed the alterations on the dress Sophia had chosen for me to wear tonight. I picked it up on my way to the salon.

Margo insisted I show her the skinny black sheath, and then decided to sweep my newly straightened hair into a sleek chignon.

"It's giving me a headache," I complained.

"The price of beauty," Marlo teased before loosening some of the pins. "Sophia did nothing but talk about your paintings. Good luck tonight."

"Thanks. At least I'll know I look good."

"That you will," Marlo said.

Max wasn't home when I returned. He'd left a note stuck to the refrigerator.

Mom I'm meeting friends for drinks. I'll see you at the gallery. You're going to be a hit. Love Max

In spite of knowing how good these paintings were, butterflies still tap danced in my stomach. My hands shook as I pulled the black patent stilettos from the box, slipped them onto my feet, and stood before the mirror.

I'd certainly come a long way from the rebellion of the sixties and seventies, women's lib, ripped jeans and bra-burning. A long ways forward or a long ways back? Right now I didn't know.

Still playing surrogate girlfriend, Sophia insisted on sending her car and driver to my tiny Queen Anne bungalow to pick me up. I felt sorry for the poor guy as he spent fifteen minutes trying to turn the stretch Towncar around on the narrow dead-end street.

By the time I arrived, the gallery was over half full, with more crowding in. Rather than make a grand entrance I slipped in the backdoor unnoticed.

Reynolds Gallery openings were a place to be seen as much as to see what the artists had produced. So I expected the room to be buzzing with the usual din of chattering and clinking glasses. Instead people moved from one painting to the next, talking quietly as if they were in a church, except for the touching. I smiled as I noticed the number of men who felt it necessary to remove their jackets to cover erections.

A small crowd of women had gathered in the alcove where I'd displayed the pictures of Teros along with the study of his various body parts. Awe lit their faces as if they'd been touched by something godly. Brass stanchions and a velvet rope kept people a safe distance from the still wet mother and son. They still crowded close to it, leaning over the velvet barrier as if drawn to the painting.

Sophia walked over. "Serena, you look marvelous, and I've already sold Moonlight Couple and the mountain landscape. There's also serious interest in the mother and son."

"It's not finished."

"They know that. I think the anticipation of its completion is what's driving the interest."

Sophia moved in closer and whispered in my ear. "After you left last night I got to thinking we'd greatly undervalued these new works. So I doubled the asking prices. Hope you don't mind."

"I don't mind," I said in shock.

"Don't worry," Sophia said. "Judging from the response so far, I could've tripled them."

"You're kidding."

"Not, at all. Isn't it marvelous?" Sophia sounded giddy.

"Thanks for everything," I gave her a brief hug.

"I'm just looking out for my own very selfish interests," she said.

A photographer came up. "Ms. Reynolds and Ms. Davies, can I get a photo for the Sunday section?"

"Of course," Sophia said.

We looped our arms around each other's waists and smiled into the camera.

"Time for you to get to work," Sophia said when the reporter left. "Michael always said you were one of few artists who can sell as well as they create. If you're half as good as he said, we are going to make a lot of money tonight." Sophia spotted someone and hurried away to greet them.

"Serena! Oh my god, woman you're a stone fox," Danielle said.

Danielle looked fabulous in a low cut black dress that showed off her considerable cleavage. May also looked stunning, in a sheer red silk top with a black lace camisole underneath and skinny black pants. Both women sported heels even higher than the ones Sophia had insisted I wear.

I couldn't believe how much I'd missed them. We stood around hugging until we were all in tears.

"Wow!" May said looking me up and down. "Who knew?"

"Makeover. You know, like one of those television shows," I said.

"Well you look great. Your paintings look even better here. I really love the ones you did after we left." May said.

"This is the best show I've ever been to. Have you sold the painting of us yet?" Danielle asked.

"Not yet."

"Great. May invited a friend who's visiting from Hong Kong. We think she'll want to buy it. How much?"

"One never discusses the price of one's art," I said.

Danielle laughed. "Yeah sure you don't. So can one assume the art is pricey?"

"Sixteen," I said, actually finding it pretty hard to believe myself. Eight thousand had seemed a bit out of reach when Sophia and I initially discussed pricing.

"Bargain!" May said. "We should get a commission or something!"

"Hey everybody, is this where the camp reunion is?" Henry walked over, looking dapper in a grey sports coat.

I suddenly realized although I'd spent a lot of time with these people, I'd never seen them in anything other than jeans, shorts and tee shirts.

"Heck yes," May said, hugging him.

"Is Priscilla here?" I asked.

He nodded. "She's standing in front of our painting. I haven't been able to get her to move." Henry looked around, and then said, "Don't mention it, but I'm surprising her with it as a wedding gift."

"You two are getting married? Congratulations. This calls for a toast." I waved over the waiter and we all took champagne glasses from the tray.

"To Henry and Priscilla, many happy years of loving and fucking," May said.

I couldn't be sure, but beneath his dark chocolate skin, I think Henry actually blushed.

"Here, here," he said.

I left them talking, mostly about how great an artist I am. Priscilla stood before the picture of her and Henry.

"Congratulations or is it best wishes to the bride? Henry told me you two are getting married."

"Thank you." She swiped a hand over her cheek wiping away tears. "It's entirely your fault, you know. This bloody gorgeous painting showed us the love we hadn't been able to contemplate. Hell, I thought we were just having a fling." She hugged me. "I haven't seen Teros, yet."

"We were just having a fling," I said. Unshed tears formed a painful lump in my throat.

"That saddens me. You two seemed so perfect together."

"I'm really happy for you and Henry."

We hugged again, and I hurried away before I could do something foolish like start bawling.

Circulating through a room filled with horny people can be quite an experience, although the most disconcerting part had to be feeling this vibe coming off my own son.

Max leaned down to kiss my cheek.

"Geez Mom! This is a great show."

He'd wrapped one arm around the waist of a pretty, dark haired woman, who looked familiar. My staid psychologist son also appeared to be playing with her butt.

"You remember Nina, don't you?"

Max and Nina had dated his first year of graduate school.

"Of course, how are you?" I asked.

"I'm good, but you look terrific and your paintings are breathtaking."

"Thanks."

Another college friend of Max's wandered over. I took the opportunity to excuse myself.

As I walked around the corner, I spotted her and Him! Something about Nola Garrett had changed. She looked dazzling. And him, oh my god, positively gorgeous, sexy as hell and hung like a horse. Where in the world had she found him? I felt my libido revving in spite of my despair over Teros.

"Nola!" I hurried into her outstretched arms. After she released me, I did a slow turn letting her get the full affect. "So what do you think?" I asked.

"Serena, you look fabulous. What happened to the landscapes?"

"I call it my sexual reawakening." I glanced over at him. His eyes were on Nola and everything about him looked ready to fuck her brains out. Good for her.

Nola made the introductions.

"Serena, this is my uh, um - neighbor, Amon"

Amon, an unusual name, but it seemed to fit him. When he took my hand a shot of electricity went straight to my pussy. Wow, really good for Nola.

"I'll let you two catch up." He walked away, but kept his eyes on Nola.

"These are wonderful," Nola said. "You have to tell me what happened at that retreat."

"Lots of healthy eating, long walks, time to paint and reflect and one extremely sexy, young associate art professor who got me to explore the real subjects of all those yearning landscapes and provocative still lifes that I used to paint."

"Well, you started exploring something alright. These are incredibly hot."

I laughed. We'd had some pretty wild days in college, but Nola had been married over thirty years before her divorce. My show had to be freaking her out, though not as much as I thought it would. Must be him.

"Yeah, makes you want to get naked and nasty, doesn't it? Speaking of naked and nasty, are there any more at home like him? Sex practically oozes off that man."

How cute. At her age Nola actually looked embarrassed to talk about sex.

"You know," I said. "If you'd asked me ten minutes ago, I'd say nothing beats the sexual energy of a younger man. But looking at him makes me think I might be very much mistaken."

Nola bristled, but said nothing.

"Down girl, let me show you what I've done." Linking her arm through mine, I led her through the exhibition. Amon followed at a discreet distance.

"Oh my god, I'm going to need a cold shower after this," Nola joked.

"Not with him," I looked over in his direction.

He'd stopped in front of the painting of Teros, a curious expression on his handsome face.

"When he looks at you he's thinking one thing."

"What's that?" Nola asked.

"Tonight, I'm going to fuck this woman over and over."

"I think your young professor has given you sex on the brain."

"True, but it doesn't change the facts for you, little sister. It's all right there, in the way he stands and in that enormous bulge which, unlike every other man, he's not even trying to hide."

Nola looked as if she would choke, so I pushed it a bit further. What are best friends for? "That bulge in his pants is for you, baby."

Had it been that long for her? I mean she'd told me she and her ex, Jack were not interested any longer. Amon looked over, catching me staring and smiled. This was definitely not the case with him.

Suddenly my longing for Teros became a physical pain. I sucked in a deep breath. Nola looked at me sharply. I shook my head. I couldn't talk about it now, or I'd break down. Nola gave my arm a squeeze that said she'd be there when I could. What are best friends for?

"Is your young professor here? I'd love to meet this miracle man."

"No, he couldn't make it." I lied. And from the look Nola gave me, I knew she knew it.

Amon wandered back, slipping his arm around Nola's waist.

"You're very talented," he said.

"Thank you. I love to watch people's reaction to my work. I got the feeling something about my paintings bothered you."

"To the contrary, they reminded me of a wonderful period in my past. They are truly great expressions of love." His gazed rested on Nola.

Tears pooled in my eyes. I brushed them way feeling like an idiot. "What extraordinary insight. You should think about buying one of my paintings."

"I might do that, although when you have the real thing, all else pales."

He pulled Nola closer.

"Would you consider allowing me to paint you?" I meant nude of course. His smile said he knew that. A flood of heat engulfed me and started a wet stream between my legs.

"Of course, as long as Nola wouldn't mind," Amon said.

I didn't have time to hear her response as Geoffrey and his husband Mason came over.

"Serena Davies, shame on you. We can't decide which one to buy and you know we can't afford them all," Geoffrey said.

"You'd be surprised at the deals I can make," I told them, then said to Nola. "Gotta get to work. Nola, enjoy tonight, you're way overdue."

"I should have two cups for coffee unpacked by tomorrow and I'm expecting you to be my first guest," Nola said.

"Count on it. I'm guessing you're going to want me to call ahead?"

"Of course, but don't' make me come looking for you."

"I won't, promise."

Geoffrey and Mason quibbled back and forth as I refereed. It took some time, but they finally decided on the study of Teros' body parts.

I left them arguing about where they would hang them in their Mercer Island mini-mansion.

I passed Sophia in the hall headed for her office with a well-dressed, much younger man in tow.

"The critics, the buyers even the lookers, went absolutely berserk for you. If you stop by the office before you go home? I'll give you a quick update."

My feet ached and the sheath felt as uncomfortable as a sausage casing, but I didn't have the heart to tell her no.

"Sure, let me grab my purse first," I said.

I found Sophia and the man inside her office making out like crazy.

"Oops," she said. Sophia hopped off her desk and straightened her dress.

"Serena, I want you to meet my friend, Neal."

"Hello, it's nice to meet you. You've got a little," I brushed my lip to indicate the smudge of Sophia's lipstick on his face.

"Oh, yeah thanks. Serena, your stuff is great. Sophia is helping me decide which one to buy."

"Then I certainly don't want to interrupt"

"I took offers on two of the landscapes and there is a small bidding war going on for the picture of the two women and it's already reached almost twice the asking."

"Great."

"You look beat. I'll walk you out. Be right back," she called over her shoulder to Neal.

"He's cute isn't he?" she asked when we were out of Neal's hearing.

"Yes, he's cute in a Clark Kent kind of way."

"Don't look so shocked. After all you're the one who opened my eyes to the possibilities. Did I mention he's also as rich as God? I did a background check and had his credit report run."

"A background check and a credit report? The rich really are different aren't they?"

Sophia laughed at this, and then her expression turned serious. "So how are you doing? Are you going to be okay? This is just the start, you know."

"I'm going to be fine."

"Good because I've got big plans for us." Sophia gave me a hug and tucked me into the luxurious backseat of her limo.

"Get some rest. I'll call you."

At home, I started the water in the bath tub; I kicked off the pumps, peeled out of the dress, and extracted the bobby pins from my scalp, promising my feet and the rest of my body I'd never torture it like that again.

I eased down into the lavender and vanilla scented bubbles. Since Teros hadn't been far from my thoughts all evening, bringing his face, his body and the feel of him inside me to the forefront took no effort.

Eyes closed I recalled the baths where I sat on muscular thighs and hard cock. His hands played with the suds on my breasts, tweaking the nipples until I whimpered with need. He'd kissed me, and then kissed me again until I couldn't breathe.

"I'm here to serve you, so tell me what you want Serena," he whispered in my ear.

I pressed against him.

"Deeper, I want to feel your cock filling me up until there's no room for anything else."

Miraculously he complied, growing bigger inside me.

"Yes, that's it. Now move."

Teros would grip my ass, pumping himself in and out. Everything inside me tightened to hold onto the memory of a perfect fuck. Teros' rough finger tips tickled my clit squeezing it gently.

His voice whispered. "What do you want?"

I didn't answer the voice in my head. He squeezed my clit tighter, sending a warm flood into the water. I'm here to serve you. Tell me what you want, Serena."

"A life time of this," I said aloud. "But I can't."

Deliberately I pushed away these thoughts. How could a memory be so insistent? Could wanting him so badly be making me a little crazy? Shaken, I flipped the drain lever with my toe and climbed from the tub, wrapping myself in the bath towel. Masturbating to thoughts of Teros had definitely been a bad idea. Now I really felt like crap.

I didn't bother with a tee shirt, climbing naked between the cool sheets. I swallowed two of the sleeping pills Sophia had given me with firm instructions to take only one at a time. I turned out the light.

His lips against mine woke me, and I wrapped my arms around Teros' naked body, feeling his erection press between my thighs.

"Hmm," I groaned. "Why are you here? "

"I missed burying my cock in your heat, and feeling your breath against my chest, sucking your clit, and tasting you against my tongue when you come. I miss the feel of your breast in my mouth, and that sound you make when you're almost ready. I missed fucking you, Serena, and I know you have missed fucking me."

"We shouldn't do this. It will only make things harder."

I pressed against him beneath the covers and could feel him smiling in the darkness.

"This is only a dream Serena, so you can tell me to go away."

Feeling him this close I couldn't deny my desire.

"Since it's only a dream, stay."

Without another word he slid his head beneath the covers. I thought I'd have a heart attack, as his tongue lapped at my pussy.

"You taste sweet, like honey," he whispered around a mouth full of clit. "Tell me what you want."

"You, I want you Teros. But I'll settle for this dream. Make me come."

Teros obliged lifting me gently he kissed my pussy then opened it wide and blew in his warm breath. My blood caught fire with need.

When Teros entered me, nothing could have been more real. I allowed myself this fantasy holding my orgasm at bay.

Then Teros surprised me, by lifting my butt and sliding a finger between my cheeks. As his finger moved deeper, I came almost immediately, feeling my whole body and soul turn inside out, muscles stripped bare, clenching around his fingers as the waves of pleasure beyond pleasure washed over me.

Love and desire for him consumed me. I squeezed tight around his cock, urging him on.

His breathing grew quick and I rubbed my hands down the sweat slicked muscles of his back. Rising onto his knees he grabbed my hips and forced himself deeper with every stroke.

"God, I love you," I whispered.

"I love you too Serena," Teros said, as his body shook with orgasm.

I came again, feeling our fluids mix inside me.

"Oh god I forgot the condom," I said.

Teros laughed. "This is only a dream."

Then he came again. For a second time Teros cum rushed into me overwhelming my senses making me drunk with joy and dizzy with happiness. I gasped, thrashing my head against the pillow trying to stop the spinning inside my head.

A bright light stabbed through my eyelids and pictures flashed before my eyes.

The Teros of that first drawing on the beach, laurel wreath, short chiton, sandals and a bow, walked through a temple toward a beautiful young woman. She laid flowers before a statute of him. Teros walked up behind her, wrapping his arms around her waist. Then he kissed her slender neck. She turned with a smile on her lips. Their love for each other showed on their faces. Teros lowered his head to capture her lips with his own. A pang of jealousy tightened my gut as their tongues entwined.

The scene changed and the woman lay on a pallet on the floor of hut, her belly large with new life. She writhed and screamed in labor. Teros knelt beside her, holding her hand in his. She screamed again. Her dark eyes were filled with pain and fear. Another pain wracked her slight body and she shook violently. Her blood soaked the pallet. The hot coppery smell mixed with the odors of her sweat and fear. The woman gripped Teros hand her face contorted in pain and then it relaxed. She smiled up weakly at him before her eyes closed. Her lifeless, hand fell from his.

Tears streaming down his face, Teros raged through the tiny hut, breaking what little furniture it held. He kicked down the door and raced outside. When he raised his hands to the sky dark clouds covered the sun. He pointed a finger and lightening cracked the sky. The hut burst into flames.

I bolted upright in my bed.

"What in the world?"

Okay maybe more than a little crazy.

Chapter Twelve

Groping through the mound of covers, I managed to free my hand and grab the telephone.

"Hello?"

"Serena, I hope I didn't wake you, but I couldn't wait to tell you I accepted a huge offer on your mother and son from a gallery in Paris. "

"Great."

"Oh, it's better than great. Your show has put The Reynolds Gallery on the international scene with a bullet. I've got a reporter from Art Internationalé coming to take pictures next week, and they want to interview you. How's your French?"

"Awful,"

"Oh well, it probably doesn't matter. The person who called spoke English. You don't sound good, are you sure you're alright? "

God, what were those pills she'd given me? And why couldn't she stop talking and give me a minute to wake up?

"I'm sorry Sophia, can I call you back?"

She gasped. "Yes of course. I forget the rest of the world does not necessarily rise with the sun." Sophia giggled. "Fortunate for me, Neal is a morning person"

I hung up the phone on whatever else she wanted to say. My head fell back against the pillows with a thud.

What time is it? Almost nine o'clock. Damn, I'd promised Nola and she wasn't going to take no for an answer. I dialed her number.

"Nola, how about I give you two hours of dedicated unpacking a couple of hours from now?"

"Perfect. Just wake up?"

"Yeah."

"See you in a couple of hours or so."

That's the good thing about longtime friends, not a lot of conversation necessary. Although, later she would press me for what happened at St. Catherine's.

Max knocked on the bedroom door.

"Come in."

My handsome 31 year-old son walked in and leaned down to kiss my cheek. The smell of freshly brewed coffee wafted from the mug in his hand. The smile on his face told me he and Nina had gotten reacquainted last night. He brushed a stray lock of hair from his eyes, reminding me of the little boy who used to race in every morning and jump onto my bed. Now he had a thriving practice and a tenure track position at a prestigious university. Not bad for a single mother.

"Mom, your show completely blew me and everyone else there away. I can't believe – I mean nobody thinks of that much sex and their Mom – I don't know how to say it. Except those paintings are your absolute best. When Teros raved about how good you are, I had no idea."

The mention of Teros name started my heart pounding. Max watched knowingly.

"As your son, I'd say you're as in love with him as he is with you. As a psychologist, I'd tell you that unresolved issues are the basis of most mental illness."

"And as your mother, I'd say butt out."

Max smiled that little boy smile. "Your touchiness just supports what I've been saying. Here." He handed me the mug. "It looks as if you could use this more than me."

"Thank you son." I took a sip, feeling the hot brew start to clear the cobwebs.

"Dinner tonight," Max called over his shoulder.

"Sure, I'll cook." I said.

"Not unless you've improved. I'll make reservations."

I fell back again, careful to keep the cup steady. I'd better get moving pretty soon, if I was going to get to Nola's before eleven.

I heard the front door open and shut, took another sip of the brew, and flipped back the covers. The hot coffee backed up in my throat as I looked down at a glistening sheen of what looked like cum coating my thighs.

"I'm Serena Davies, here to see Nola Garrett," I told the doorman whose desk stood between me and the elevators to the upper floors.

"Of course, Ms. Davies, she said to send you right up."

"Of course."

I smiled at him and he smiled back. If he noticed my sarcasm he didn't give any indication. Tower A was some posh place.

Nola answered the door looking like she'd won the lottery of sexual gratification. The woman literally beamed as she pulled me into a hug.

"Talkin' about moving on up. This place is awesome."

Nola beamed some more.

"Yeah it is. I just found out Amon is the architect."

"Get outta here, talented and hot as hell. You've got it made, girl."

"You might be right. Want some coffee?"

"I'd love some. By the way, where is Mr. Sex on a Stick?"

Looking out the window at the sweeping view of Puget Sound and the city, I followed her over to the most beautiful blue marble counter I'd ever seen. Okay, now I was officially leaf green with envy.

"Amon had a meeting this morning. He'll be back around one o'clock."

I hadn't seen Nola blush in at least two decades. Now it seemed she couldn't stop as she gushed over the contents of the Victoria's Secret housewarming gift I picked up on the way over.

"Is he as good as he looks?" I asked, half expecting to get some vague answer.

"Do you remember the multiple orgasm contest of our junior year?" Nola asked.

"I remember winning it."

"Well last night I blew your record out of the water, sister."

"Whoa, good for you. How'd you do after such a long dry spell?"

"I thought I'd be horrible at it, but with him…" Her voice trailed off into a widening smile.

"Check out the rest of your gift. I put my doctor's card in the bottom. Dr. Blessing specializes in women getting back into the saddle as it were."

"Somebody actually specializes in that?" Nola asked incredulous.

"Hey, from what I've heard, there can be complications."

"I'll give her call."

Unpacking boxes and talking about Nola's sexual exploits kept my mind off Teros and last night's disturbing dream. Nola handed me a box of memorabilia to unwrap.

"Tell me about him," Nola demanded.

"You saw what he looks like. He helped me grow as an artist and a person in ways I'd never have imagined."

"So far so good," Nola said.

"And having sex with him is so phenomenal it almost frightens me."

Nola's look said she understood this from experience, most likely very recent experience.

"What are the warts?" she asked.

"He teaches art at the same school with Max."

"Teros, what an unusual name."

"He's Greek. It's short for Anteros."

"So, are we talking about a summer booty call, or something deeper?" Nola asked. I could tell from the sound of her voice, she knew it went deeper, much deeper, and she wanted me talk it through.

"Did you ever think we'd be in a position to be called cougars?"

"No, what's that?"

"Well you're not. How old is Amon?"

"I don't know. I haven't asked yet."

"Well Teros is probably less than five years older than Max."

"So, I take it he's in love with you too?"

"Yes. At least he is now. You remember how we used to change our minds at that age?"

"I remember how often you changed men at that age. I'd gotten married."

"Why couldn't there be another Amon?"

Nola shot me a don't-even-think-about-it-look.

"Not him. I meant another man who is gorgeous, sexy and age appropriate."

"Let me make sure I understand this. You've found a man who loves you, loves your work, who is supportive and who is a phenomenal- your word, not mine, lover, but he's somehow not good enough for you?" Nola laughed. "My Serena Davies; how your standards have changed."

"You wouldn't be the one enduring the disapproving looks and snide comments," I said hearing my voice crack.

"It never mattered before."

I opened my mouth to protest.

Nola rolled her eyes. "As long as I've known you Serena other people's opinions of you did not matter. Between your wild hair, artsy clothes, and sending your son to a Hebrew day school, when you're a Catholic, you flat out didn't give a damn about what other people thought."

"I wanted Max to be well rounded," I said.

"How about that Volkswagen Van you drove all over town after painting it Pepto Bismol pink and tacking varnished brassieres all over the outside."

"An artistic and political statement about the objectification of women."

"I got it. How about when you carried baby Max around on a papoose back board? Need I go on?"

"Okay, so it's easier to be a non-conformist when you're young."

"I don't think so. You're still a non-conformist. I just think you're afraid of opening yourself up to loving someone again," Nola said.

"You're an engineer, not a psychologist. I've got a son for that."

"So what does Max think?"

I hesitated. Her eyebrows rose.

"He thinks I should go for it," I admitted.

"I rest my case. You know it takes a very smart woman to know when she's met that right person."

"So?" I said sarcastically.

"Think about it Serena. We were among the first generation of American women who said screw it and did. We made out-in-the-open choices about sex and life."

Nola came over and wrapped an arm around my shoulders. "Put on your big girl panties and just say screw it. I'm in love with this man, and he just happens to be younger than me."

"You think it's that easy."

"No, but I think you'll regret it for the rest of your life if you don't." Nola said.

I looked down at the watch my son had given me for my 45th birthday. "I better get out of here, it's almost one."

"Sorry, where did the time go? I don't want to rush you." Nola retrieved my shawl from the hall tree and wrapped it over my shoulders herding me toward the door.

I laughed at her obvious anxiousness. "Sure you don't."

"You still owe me a half-hour too, but I'll take a rain check." She opened the door.

"Okay, I'm leaving before you throw me out," I teased her.

The elevator dinged and the doors opened. Amon strode down the hallway looking amazing and sexy in a black suit and white shirt with blue tie, and an obvious erection.

Without a word he pulled my best friend into his arms. Pressing her back against the door jamb he delivered a kiss so hot it could've melted the tasteful brass light sconces.

God, I miss that and damn it I want it back!

Finally he released her mouth, but his arms remained entwined around her. Nola probably required holding up. I knew I would after a kiss like that.

He turned as if noticing me for the first time.

"Sorry Serena, I needed that," Amon said with a sexy smile.

"Me too. I'll see you later Nola, I've got a call to make."

"Good. How about we do yoga on Tuesday? We can go out to breakfast afterwards and catch up some more."

"Tuesday then." I headed for the elevator, while they began tearing at each other's clothes. "Remarkable building, Amon," I called over my shoulder.

"Thank you," he said.

I heard the door slam.

Downstairs, I stopped at one of the bars off the lobby and took a table away from the business lunch crowd.

A pretty young waitress parked at the edge of the table. "What can I get for you?" she asked.

"Dirty martini, three olives."

She nodded and walked back to the bar. While I waited, I used the time to admire Amon's remarkable architecture and tried not to think about what he and Nola were undoubtedly doing at this moment.

The waitress returned, setting my drink on the table. After a bracing sip of the cool elixir, I'd managed to calm my screaming libido and pulled out my cell phone.

The message box showed I had a call from Sophia. I'd call her back later.

It took some doing, but I finally worked my way through the university's phone tree to Teros' line. A battle waged between mind and heart; hoping the phone would just ring and wanting him to answer.

"Hello Serena."

My pussy flooded at the sound of his voice.

"Teros, I've been thinking. I mean if it's not too late. We should—"

"I give my last mid-term Monday night, so I'll be there on Tuesday morning. I couldn't get an earlier flight."

Relief and desire washed over me. "I miss you," I whispered into the phone.

"I love you and I miss fucking you," Teros said quietly.

Reaching for the martini, I took another sip, to blunt my raging lust. "I love you too."

"Good. That's one thing we won't have to fight about."

I heard the smile in his voice and smiled too.

The waitress brought over another martini, setting it down in front of me.

I gave her a puzzled look.

"From the gentleman at the bar," she said tilting her head in that direction.

Michael Reynolds lifted his glass in a salute.

"Excuse me a minute Teros." I covered the cell's mouthpiece, pulled a twenty from my purse, and set it next to the drink. "Take it back. Keep the change and please tell the gentleman, I said go to hell," I instructed her.

The woman looked ecstatic. With a wicked smile she retrieved the money and second martini. "Thank you, and by the way, I would have delivered your message for free."

What a classless jerk. He'd probably been hitting on her since he stepped in the door.

"I'm back. Did you want me to pick you up at the airport?" I asked Teros.

"I'll get a taxi. I wish I could leave now, hearing your voice has given me a rampant hard on."

At the sound of his heavy breathing, even more lust ripped through my gut, and settled between my legs. I squirmed on the rich velvet seat. "I wish you could too. By the way, I had the strangest dream about you the other night."

"Talking to the new man?" Michael stood over me. "I could always tell when you were getting hot. You get this smoky look in those bedroom eyes of yours."

"I'm sorry Teros, I have to take care of something. Can I call you right back?"

"Class is about to start and I've got to take care of something or suffer permanent injury."

"We wouldn't want that," I couldn't stop myself from giggling.

"I'll make you pay for that," Teros threatened.

"How about later tonight on the phone?" I asked as thoughts of his repayment made me wetter.

"Sorry babe. Between the installation of Aphrodite and classes, I'll be pretty much tied up until my plane leaves, but it's only a couple of days. We'll both have to suffer."

Michael stood next to the table hanging on every word.

"Good, I'll see you soon. Did you need directions?"

"I always know where you are. And now thanks to you, I'm going to have to jerk off before my next lecture."

I laughed aloud at that. "Think of me."

"Of course," he said.

I heard him kiss the phone before the line went dead.

"It's rude to eavesdrop," I said glaring at Michael.

"You look fabulous Serena." Michael leaned in to kiss me. Before his lips reached mine, our eyes locked in a brief battle. I won. He straightened.

Why I'd ever thought he was someone I might fall in love with was a complete mystery. How could I have failed to notice that cold, selfish look in his gray eyes or the cruelness about his too thin lips?

"Your showing nearly gave me a heart attack."

"Too bad only nearly."

Michael chuckled. "Don't be a hater. Mind if I sit down? We've got some catching up to do."

"By all means, sit."

As he slid into the booth I slid out the other side.

"Gotta go. I would say have a nice life, but I really don't give a damn if you do or you don't."

He reached out and stroked a hand down my arm. "Come on Serena, I swear I only want to talk about business."

"I thought the gallery belongs to Sophia."

"It does, but I'm working on opening a new space." Michael said.

"How nice for you. Good luck with that. "

He changed tack. "You're actually my discovery and for the prices Sophia is getting for your new stuff, I think I'm owed a piece."

"A piece?" I burst out laughing.

People turned to stare. "Why in the world would you think I owe you anything, because you're such a dazzlingly good fuck? Not hardly, Michael."

He at least had the decency to look contrite.

"You're a selfish bastard in bed and out."

"Can't we be adult about this? My attorney said if you signed an affidavit saying that we had a verbal agreement and that I supported this tremendous escalation in the value of your work —"

"If I what? Hmm, how can I put this nicely? Hell no. Not if your sorry life depended on it."

"Serena, please! " He raked his hand through that famous silver head of hair. "We had feelings for each other."

"Michael, let me give you the same 'piece' of advice you once gave me. Fucking is fucking and business is business."

"I'll fight you over this!" Michael called.

It took every bit of my self control not to go back smack him upside the head. "So fight me. I'll relish kicking your ass." I walked out of the bar.

My world couldn't have looked better. I'd put the ghost of Michael to rest and more importantly Teros would be here on Tuesday!

Chapter Thirteen

"He applied for an assistant professor position at Seattle U," Max said, watching me vacuum my cozy living room for the fourth time.

"What, why?"

"Because he's in love with you and wants to be near you. That's what people in love do. It's kind of like cleaning your house incessantly."

I swallowed down the rising panic.

"What if it doesn't work out? He's giving up a better position at a more prestigious university."

I grabbed the dust rag and began circling the picture frames again.

"I don't want that burden."

"Mom, he's a grown man and it's his choice. Stop with the guilt," my psychologist son chided. "Besides I can tell, Teros is not just another one of your flings."

"Are you too old to send to your room?"

"Yes, and I've got a plane to catch." Max came over and hugged me. "I'll be back for Thanksgiving. You should let Aunt Nola cook this year. She's much better at it."

"Thank you, son. You should settle down with someone and invite me for Thanksgiving."

From the doorway I watched my son drive away in his rented Mustang convertible.

Inside my studio my latest piece stood on the easel. I picked up the charcoal pencil and went to work. George and Agnes slowly came to life beneath the crystalline spray of the water fall. This would be the last painting in the series.

I could recall how everything surrounding the couple had curved sensually, water droplets, vegetation, juts and crags of the rock formation covered in lush velvet moss, mimicking the couple's entwined bodies. Until I'd put on the canvas in front of me, I hadn't realized how perfect composition had been when I'd come upon them. Now I could blame it on being totally overwhelmed by the Agnes' unearthly splendor.

The doorbell rang. Glancing out the window I saw Sophia's Porsche Boxster parked behind my old Volvo.

"I came over to 'check up' on you. You seemed a little down." Sophia stared at my face. "But something has changed."

"I'm working on a new piece. This will be the last in the series. Come on back and see it."

We stopped in the kitchen. I poured two glasses of wine and led the way to my studio.

"This is fabulous," she said sipping from her wine glass. "I may buy it for my own collection."

"Thanks."

"The couple is hot, but it's the woman I really love."

"Why?"

"It's all that unbelievable wisdom and confidence you've put in her eyes. " Sophia said. "I want to be her when I grow up. Everything you paint is spectacular, but you've broken out with the eyes. They are profound."

All night Monday I tossed and turned, anxious for Teros arrival. Fear and excitement were waging a fierce competition for my nerves. A little after five o'clock, I gave up trying to sleep and crawled out of bed.

I'd promised to meet Nola for yoga class, although if she didn't make it I wouldn't be surprised. She wasn't there when I arrived. Unrolling my mat at the back of the room, I left the front spaces for those more serious about the practice.

We'd just started the ohms when Nola slipped in the back door and unrolled her mat next to mine. I glanced at her sideways. She looked different, younger. But one look in her eyes and I knew something wasn't right.

"Ohmmm. Glad you could make it."

"Ohmmm, me too," she said.

By the end of the warm up poses I'd stopped thinking about Teros, and worried about what was up with Nola instead.

"Lie flat on your stomachs. Reach back and grab hold of your ankles. Deep inhale and hold the breath in. Move up into bow pose," the instructor said. The assistant instructor moved through the room adjusting legs and arms and pushing down on shoulders. She stopped in front of Nola.

"Very good Nola. It seems you had a breakthrough."

I nearly choked on the laughter that bubbled up. Fucking like a rabbit could probably lead to all sorts of breakthroughs.

"We should all be lucky enough to have a breakthrough like yours," I whispered.

"Shhh!" Nola hissed back, sounding upset.

Had she and Amon had their first fight?

"Namaste'" the class said in unison, bowing.

We began rolling our mats up. "So you want to grab some breakfast, or is someone keeping the bed warm for you?" I asked. Nola looked embarrassed.

"No, I've got time. Besides it's been a while since we just hung out. We should do a spa day go for facials and pedicures or get a massage."

Why did she want to go to a spa with Amon at home?

We walked to our favorite breakfast place.

"I thought you were getting plenty of massages from him. Besides, I can't, I'm expecting Teros to show up any minute."

"Then shouldn't you be home?" Nola asked. "We can do breakfast another time."

"No, he'll find me here. And I'm anxious for you to meet him."

I loaded my plate from the steam table with eggs Florentine, glancing sidelong at Nola. She looked beautiful, almost ethereal. "Wow, you're practically glowing," I told her.

She shrugged it off and pulling out her wallet at the cashier. "My treat."

"No, you always treat. Let me get this one."

The cashier looked impatiently over our heads at the rest of the line. I let Nola pay.

"I'm not a starving artist any more. You'd never know the economy had taken a dive from the sales of my new paintings."

"I'd like to buy that island landscape myself," Nola said.

"You'll have to get in line. I've sold it and almost everything else. The asking prices bordered on obscene and at least two sold for more. I actually overheard someone referring to them as investment pieces."

"I don't find it surprising. You were always good, but now you've reached a whole different level and not just because of the subject matter."

I led the way to our usual booth in the back.

"Don't you want to sit out front where Teros will see you?" Nola asked.

"He'll find me. He always does. It's almost spooky. When I tried to give him my address, he said he didn't need it "

"Maybe you'd given it to him before, or Max had."

"Maybe."

I knew I hadn't but trying to explain that would just make me sound crazy. Besides I wanted to hear what happened between her and Amon.

"So what's bugging you and don't try to lie? You're bad at it and I'll see right through you."

As her guard dropped, I could see how really upset she was. "I'm going to stop seeing Amon," she said slowly.

"Why in the world would you do that? Have you looked in the mirror? You look happier than I've ever seen you before. Ever! You and Amon had a fight didn't you?"

Nola shook her head. "It's more complicated than that."

"I'm good with complicated," I said taking her hand. "Talk."

Her expression crumpled and tears rolled down her cheeks. Nola swore wiping at them with the paper napkin. "I really can't talk about it right now, she said.

I got mad. Nola was not crying type. Whatever Amon had said or done had to be pretty bad.

The server came around and we both flipped our coffee mugs upright.

Nola would eventually tell me. I only hoped that would happen before Teros arrived.

"Did you make an appointment with Dr. Blessing yet?" I asked.

"No. I don't seem to be having any problems."

"Go in anyway. I wouldn't want you to rupture anything, like a woman I met at the retreat. She had this absolute horror story about tearing something and bleeding internally."

"Hey, I'm trying to eat here!" Nola said.

"Sorry. It's just that she told me she needed these special titanium stitches and then——"

"Stop! I'll go see your doctor okay?"

Knowing about Nola's illness phobia I already had my cell phone out. "Good. I actually made that up. So why don't you call her now? You know you look fantastic, but something is definitely different."

I hit Dr. Blessing listing from my phonebook and handed the telephone to Nola. She looked as if she didn't want to take it. Too bad. Frowning, she finally snatched it from my hand.

Nola talked for a minute and snapped the cell phone shut, passing it back to me. "Satisfied? And what kind of doctor answers her own telephone?"

"She's a great doctor," I said. "It's still early and the reception staff probably doesn't come in until nine."

"My old doctor had a service."

"Stop bitching, I know you're just looking for an excuse to avoid climbing into those stirrups."

Suddenly a hot wave of desire washed over me and I knew he'd come. The noisy morning crowd, mostly women, fell silent.

Teros wove his way between the tables until he reached me. Leaning down he planted those exquisite lips against mine.

He lifted his head again, way too soon, and whispered "Hey babe."

For an instant I seriously thought I might not be able to stop myself from fucking him right here. He must be having similar thoughts, because he kissed me again, this time his tongue plunged into my mouth, exploring, tasting, and entwining with mine.

Every nerve exploded to life with need. Not giving a damn who might be watching, I reached up cradling his beard roughened cheeks between both hands. Teros groaned deepening his kiss even further.

That kiss lasted way longer than it should have. It took me a moment to even realize where we were when he pulled away. His green eyes burned with desire that made me wetter.

"I'm Serena's friend, Teros. Sorry, it's just that feels like a lifetime since, I've seen Serena." His deep voice washed over me, as he spoke to Nola.

"I'm Nola."

How could I ever have thought I wanted to live without feeling like this, without him?

"I really missed you too. Nola, this is Teros. Teros, Nola. Oh that's right you did that already."

He said something else to Nola. I couldn't hear it over the sound of my own heart beating in my ears. All I could think about was getting home as soon as possible to fuck him. Or maybe we could stop along the way.

"I'll call you later," Nola said and hurried off. I pushed away the brief pang of guilt. We'd talk.

"Let's go," I told Teros, knowing he understood exactly what I meant. I needed to see him naked. I needed to touch him and taste him and be fucked by him, and I needed it now.

Teros grabbed up my gym bag, slung it over one shoulder and wrapped his arm around my waist. He pulled me against the curve of his hard body. I literally quivered.

I ignored the envious and some hostile stares from several women as we left the restaurant.

Teros accepted the keys to my car. I couldn't keep my mind on the road even long enough to drive the short distance. We got into the car. He started it and squealed away from the curb.

"I heard your show went exceptionally well. Not that I harbored any doubts."

"And I owe at least part of my success to this." I unzipped his fly. That magnificent cock popped out. "I missed this too," I said taking his cock into my hands. Teros drew in a quick breath, but kept his eyes on the road.

Leaning over I swirled my tongue around the head, loving how his body shuddered.

"You know there might be some sort of law against this. How do you feel about breaking the law?" I hovered over his erect penis blowing my warm breath across it. He sucked in a ragged breath.

"Serena, please." Teros panted.

I should have stopped, but a strange sensation of power washed over me. Seeing him barely in control made me want to see just how far I could take this. I placed my lips over the pulsing head sucked gently.

"Hoh!"

Teros swerved the car into my narrow driveway and jammed on the brakes. Then he slammed back the driver's seat, stripped down my stretchy yoga pants, lifted my body and impaled my dripping pussy onto of his cock.

Thank god for roomy front seats, and yoga lessons.

"I love you," he said.

"Good, I love you too. Fuck me."

He didn't need any more encouragement. Teros began a slow pounding rhythm that touched the edge of my clit with each driving stroke. Together we ground and pounded out our passion. I could feel him growing even bigger.

Lifting up my shirt he buried his head beneath it, pushing aside the bra, and taking a breast into the heat of his mouth. I lost myself in the pleasure of him. Our breathing grew ragged. I knew he was ready to come, but he would wait for me. Not this time. I tightened my muscles on him and whispered into his ear.

"I want you to come for me, Teros."

Hot cum flooded into me.

The light show seemed to start behind my eyes and in moments engulfed me. The interior of my old Volvo disappeared into a cosmos of luminosity.

Joy, ecstasy, and the most ferocious love I'd ever experienced overwhelmed me. I clung to Teros, unable to breathe. His face glowed through the tears clouding my vision.

When I met Teros eyes he looked as shaken as I felt.

"Gods, I love you and wow, I didn't realize how much I needed to make love with you," he said burying his head in my chest."

"Me too." I laughed. "But this steering wheel is killing my back."

Teros laughed too, lifting me off his penis, gently depositing me back into the passenger seat.

"Let's go inside and do this more slowly and with a condom," I said.

Those beautiful green eyes met mine. For an instant the power behind that look, inhuman power sent a shock of fear through me. When I blinked it disappeared.

"You don't have to worry Serena. I promise," Teros whispered.

Did he mean of the unprotected sex, or of that power?

Teros mouth covered mine again. When he released me I practically ran from the car and into the house. We stripped as we went. I grabbed a condom from the night table drawer and slipped it over his stiff penis.

The rest of Tuesday and all of Wednesday we stayed in bed.

Thursday morning the telephone rang.

"Serena, are you alright?" Sophia's worried voice came through the line.

"Sophia! Oh my god, I forgot. I forgot about the releases yesterday. I'm sorry. I can be there in two hours."

"Not a problem. I'll see you soon," Sophia said.

Spooned against my back, Teros began tweaking the tips of my nipples.

"Sorry but I promised Sophia. I've got to go."

"Then I'll go with you. Now that I've seen you again, I'm not even ready to let you out of my sight."

He must have felt my sudden uneasiness. His arm tightened over me. "Everything will be alright, I promise."

This wasn't some small island with a bunch of accepting artists. This was my home, my business and people I'd known and worked with most of my life. Yet I couldn't ask Teros to pretend we weren't together, in the Biblical sense, when we went out in public. And I knew I couldn't be anywhere near him and not touch him.

I remembered Nola's sage advice. It was time to put on the big girl panties and deal with it. God knows Teros is worth it.

I rolled over to look into his handsome face.

"I wouldn't have it any other way."

Showering and dressing included kissing, touching, sucking, and Teros' cock buried inside me until we both came really loudly.

We arrived at the gallery a half hour later than what I'd promised.

"This shouldn't take long. You can walk around and see at my paintings in a proper setting," I told Teros. "There are a couple of new ones, Agnes and George and you and Agnes."

He nodded and kissed me, his tongue easing into my mouth. I surrendered any pose of not being totally affected by it and him. Lust burned in his eyes despite the fact we'd fucked right before making the drive over.

Sophia's assistant sat at her desk, mouth hanging open. I think she might have been drooling a bit.

"Sophia's expecting me." I prompted her.

"Oh, oh sorry, she's in her office."

I went back to the office and knocked on the door.

"Come in." Sophia looked flushed as she snapped her cell phone shut.

"I really am sorry I forgot to sign these earlier. Teros arrived yesterday."

"You mean the Greek god from your paintings?"

"Yes." I glanced over the release forms and signed my name.

"Tell me he's here. I'd love to meet him. Not that I'm dissatisfied with what I have right now." She gave me mischievous wink.

"He's in the gallery."

Sophia practically bolted around the desk and raced out the door.

We found Teros standing in front of the picture of his mother and him.

Sophia actually stopped and gasped. He turned around and she gasped again.

"Sophia, this is Anteros – "

She extended her hand.

"Anteros, this is Sophia Reynolds, the gallery owner."

"I naturally assumed Serena had used a certain amount of artistic license in your painting. I don't mean to be rude, but you are the most gorgeous man I have ever seen in my life."

Teros smiled.

"Serena told me you're a sculptor and you sold a piece to the Greek consulate. Do you have representation?"

"I'm actually an art professor. I don't have any completed works right now."

"I'd love to see some of your work," she went on like she hadn't heard him.

Inside my purse, my cell phone started "Let's Get It On."

I pulled it out and glanced at the number. Nola. I let it click over to voice mail.

The telephone began playing again. Nola's number.

"Excuse me. I need to take this." I called to Teros and Sophia, as I walked toward the back hall. By the time I'd answered she'd hung up. I tried to call her but the line was busy, probably leaving me a message.

Then I noticed I wasn't the only one using the hall to get some privacy. Tucked in the alcove, her back to me, Sophia's assistant had a cell phone pressed to her ear.

"You remember the guy in that picture? Well he's here in the flesh and oh-mi-god, he's fucking gorgeous," she said. "You would not believe how incredibly hot this guy is. It's almost unnatural. I mean just looking at him makes me horny. And when I saw him kissing Serena, I thought I might come right there." She paused, and then responded, "Shut up. God yes, I'd tap that in a heartbeat!"

Another long pause then, "I don't know how long they're going to be here, but you should say you're sick or something and get down here now. I've never seen anyone as totally hot as this guy is. He could sell tickets to look at him."

I heard some loud chatter coming through the phone.

"I hear you. No, he looks around 32 or so, maybe a little older, but the good kind of older. "

More chatter.

"Yeah, Serena's cool and talented, but she's got to be older than my mother."

She laughed "She does look great for a woman her age and all. But face it; a cougar is still a cougar"

The assistant grew quiet, listening.

"I hear that. Inquiring minds really want to know what would somebody as young and over-the-top, balls-to-the walls, extreme fuckalicious as him, sees in her?" She laughed again. "No, she's not rich."

I walked over and tapped her on the shoulder.

Her eyes grew wide and she began gulping air while her face turned an unflattering shade of magenta. "Yes, Ms. Davies?"

"Brittany, isn't it?"

She nodded.

"Well Brittany, I can answer that question for you."

"I'm sorry Ms. Davies. I didn't mean –"she stopped speaking.

I let her squirm a while longer in the uncomfortable silence.

"Anteros has said he's with me because he's impressed by my intelligence, mesmerized by my maturity, and even in love with my talent. But between you and me, I think it's because I'm a really, really, great fuck."

The magenta color took on a purplish cast and for a second I thought she might just pass out.

"Please Ms. Davies, I can't afford to lose this job," the assistant said.

"Don't worry about it. You wanted to know, so now I've told you."

I left her with a dumbfounded look on her face, and whoever she'd been talking to yelling into the phone on the other end.

Alrighty then, that hadn't been nearly as hard as I'd imagined.

Teros and I headed back to my car after I finally managed to pull him away from Sophia.

"You are intelligent, beautiful, enormously talented and a really, really, really, great fuck," Teros said.

"You listened, how?"

"Let's just say I heard and I love you even more. Did you talk to Nola?"

Nola ! I'd forgotten to call her back.

I listened to her message.

"Hey Serena, I've got some important news, but I'd rather tell you in person. I'll be home all afternoon. Please, please come over."

I listened to the message a second time. She sounded like she would burst if she didn't tell me this news soon. Could she and Amon be getting married, already?

How had Teros known Nola called?

His hand rubbed down my arm. I look at the bulge in his slacks and swallowed my desire. It would have to wait because Nola didn't sound like she wanted to.

Candice Butler

Chapter Fourteen

Nola answered the door, and pulled me into a hug.

"I wanted you to be the first to know."

She looked over at Amon, love clearly written all over her face. "I mean the second."

I stared at unable to believe the changes. Nola looked ten years younger and glowed like an angel. She wore an oversized top and jeans that did little to hide the fact she'd put on some weight. How, in two days?

"What's so important you had to tell me in person?" I asked.

"Come in." Amon said." Good to see you again, Anteros."

The two men shook hands and the look that passed between all three of them overflowed with subtext.

Amon moved behind Nola, encircling her with his arms.

"You'll stay for lunch." Amon said.

It wasn't a question. And the look in Nola's eyes told me she really wanted us to. So despite my anxiousness to get back to fucking Teros, I followed them into Nola's fabulous living room.

Plates and food sat atop the coffee table.

"I wanted us to be comfortable, but if you'd rather eat in the dining room?" Nola said.

"No. This is great. So what did you need to talk to me about?"

Another look passed between Teros and Amon.

"How about some wine?" Amon filled three glasses, passing one to me and Teros. "Nola and I have some very good news to share with you, after we eat."

When had Nola gone on the wagon? We helped ourselves from the array of dishes then settled down on the sofas. Amon and Teros didn't even bother with the pretense of picking at their plates.

Talk about being able to cut tension with a knife.

Nola took a couple of bites, and then excused herself to the bathroom. Both men watched her leave and looked at each other again.

I couldn't stand it any longer. "What the hell is going on?" I asked, looking from one gorgeous man to the other.

"You haven't told her." Amon said quietly.

Teros shrugged. "I guess I was waiting for the right moment."

Amon laughed. "I think this is it."

Nola returned looking a little worse for the wear.

"Okay, the food is lovely, the wine is great, but I can't enjoy any of it, until one of you tells me what all this drama is about," I said.

Amon opened his mouth to speak, but Nola put up hand. "Let me." She took a deep breath. "Don't freak out. But I'm pregnant."

"That's crazy, you can't be. You had a hysterectomy. I was the one holding the pillow when you coughed, remember?"

An angelic smile lit her face. "It grew back." Nola came and stood next to me. Turning sideways, she pulled the top tight around her middle to show off her baby bump.

"What the——" The words froze in my throat. That hadn't been there the day before yesterday! Women our age, who'd had full hysterectomies, didn't suddenly become pregnant.

"It's got to be a mistake, a hysterical pregnancy or something."

I felt myself starting to hyperventilate. Teros handed me a glass of wine.

"Drink," he ordered.

I gulped the contents half expecting the theme song to the Twilight Zone to start playing in the background.

As Nola's eyes rested on Amon, his energy seemed to reach out enveloping her in a soft glow.

"Amon is a god. The Egyptian god of fertility to be exact," she said.

"This is insane," I said.

"I didn't believe it myself, at first," Nola said. "It's true. You feel it too."

Everyone watched me, even Teros.

"Has everyone gone crazy or is the joke on me?"

"It's not a joke," Teros said.

A shaky laugh burbled up my throat.

Amon walked over taking my best friend into his arms. I watched him grind that humongous bulge against her backside, as he deposited the lightest of kisses on her neck. Nola's pupil's flared. She drew in a deep breath and sighed.

I turned to look at Teros. His green eyes locked with mine. The ancient power I'd glimpsed earlier exploded to life.

"You too?" I asked.

He reached out taking my hand.

"Sorry, babe."

Suddenly I thought I'd pass out. Raw, potent, sexuality filled that room from floor to ceiling, wall to wall, intense, all-consuming tidal waves of it rolling off both men.

Teros' hand took mine, as I felt my sanity slipping away. Lust hauled me back to reality. I fought against the urge to push him down on that sofa and fuck.

When he released my hand the desire backed off, but only a little.

"Amon is a god and he got you pregnant?" I finally managed to get out.

Nola nodded. "We're getting married." A radiant smile lit her expression.

My brain felt fogged as I looked between the two men, gods, whatever. A sheepish look replaced the power in Teros eyes.

Alone, each of them exuded a barely controllable sexuality. Together, I drowned in my need to fuck somebody, right here, right now.

How had I not guessed what Teros was before now? His cum had felt like the elixir of life pouring into me because it was quite literally the elixir of life.

Oh my god, I'd had unprotected sex with a god!

"Don't tell me Max is about to get a sibling too."

"Not unless you want another child," Teros said.

"No way! Been there, done that."

"If you're Anteros then Agnes is really—?"

"Aphrodite, yes and George is Hephaestus, the god of the forge."

"Of course, it all makes sense now. Back on the island, with all that supernatural sexual energy in the air, we poor mortals didn't stand a chance."

Teros sheepish look returned.

"It's our nature."

"And the rest of us were like lambs to the slaughter."

Overload!

All at once the floor rushed upward at my face. I felt Teros strong arms catching me and then carrying me to Nola's couch.

When I opened my eyes again, Teros leaned over me.

"It's true!" I managed to croak out.

He answered by pressing his lips to mine. I didn't try to resist the power of that kiss, god, devil, or demon. I loved him and wanted him inside me.

He finally released me from that kiss.

"Yes. Does it matter?"

I sat up, swinging my legs back to the floor and pressing them together against the desire growing inside me.

"Of course it matters," I said. "Why? why me?"

"We should leave them to work this out," Amon said to Nola.

"We'll be next door, if you need us," Nola called.

The look in Amon's eyes said they would be making good use of the time.

After the door had shut I stared at Teros beautiful face.

"The night of my show, that wasn't a dream was it?"

Teros shook his head. "I didn't mean to deceive you, but I couldn't stand to be away from you a minute longer."

"You still haven't answered, why me?"

"The first time I saw your paintings, I saw you. Your humor, your compassion, intelligence and yes your amazing sexuality. I knew I had to find you, because you did a rare thing. You fascinated me. " Teros paused. "After I met you, I knew I had to make love to you."

I blushed.

Teros smiled.

"What if —" I asked.

The undisguised hunger in his eyes silenced my question.

"You could've looked like a sea hag and I would still have loved you. Though, I may have not wanted to fuck you quite so badly."

The expression on my face must have changed because Teros laughed and added.

"I'm so glad you turned out to be one of the most beautiful women I've ever seen."

God, how I wanted him.

"The woman in the dream? Did you love her too? "

"Her name was Calla, and yes I loved her."

"So, why show her to me?"

"I didn't mean to, you—I can't explain it." Teros ran a hand down my arm. "You should know I've waited a long time to find someone else to love." He slipped his hand beneath my shirt and cradled my breast. "Does what I am change things between us?"

"Mmm, you know I can't actually think while you're doing that. Of course it changes things. You're a god. I'd be lying if I said it didn't"

His fingers sought out my nipple.

"What can I do?"

"Mmm, nothing. Lucky for you, I'm a nonconformist."

Teros pulled me into a long hot kiss.

"I'd like us to stay together, if you think you can," Teros said.

"Let's talk about that later. Right now, I'd like to—"I reached for the zipper on his pants and pulled it down, freeing that godly cock.

"Yes, later, much later." He stripped my clothes off using his mouth and hands to drive me wild.

Afterward we he rested spooned together, his magnificent cock still buried inside me. I vaguely wondered if I'd have buy Nola a new sofa or at least offer to get this one cleaned. The calloused tips of Teros fingers stroked my forehead as he moved his hips grinding his pelvis against my butt.

"How do gods live? I mean do you move in, or we, sleep on a cloud, what?"

"I hoped, after a while at least, we would live together, here. I bought a residence on the other side of the building."

I felt unbelievably happy in that moment. But fear colored that happiness. I wasn't afraid of Teros, but of what might come next. I snuggled backward.

"I'll have to think about that."

I'd lived alone a long time. I had my house and my own independence. Could I willingly give those things up for the cap left off the toothpaste, the toilet seat up and arguing about household expenses?

Teros cock grew harder and bigger. He began sliding it in and out.

"I promise we'll never argue about household expenses. We will never argue about anything," Teros said.

Okay fucking instead of fighting could work.

"Do you think Amon and Nola will be coming back soon?" I moved my hips matching his rhythm.

"I doubt it."

He chuckled.

"Amon and I are very much alike. We like to take our time. "

In one swift move Teros had his nuts securely pressed against my butt. Still slick with cum, he pressed that magnificent penis slowly in.

"Wait, wait!" I froze mid-stroke. "A thought just hit me. This means you're actually older than me, right?"

Teros laughter rumbled through his chest.

"Considerably."

Reaching between us he adjusted his angle. "If you'd like, I can look older."

"That would be easier, but I fell in love with you as you are. And that includes your fabulous looks and hard, hard body. The rest of the world will just have to deal."

"Then it's settled?"

"Except for – "

Teros needed no more encouragement.

I thrashed against the soft fabric as waves of pleasures washed over me and I tried to wait for him.

"I love you and I need to come."

Teros obliged sliding his cock deeper than I'd thought possible. He became part of me and I of him.

Next to my ear he whispered, "Come for me Serena. I'm here to serve you."

THE END

About the Author

Candice Butler, a woman of a certain age, is a former investigator. She is a member of Romance Writers of America and its Passionate Ink chapter. She lives and writes in Seattle, Washington, and in her house by the Pacific, with her husband and one cat. This is her first book in the Oh My Gods Series. "Because we are never too old for passion."

To learn more about Candice and find more books visit www.candicebutler.com.

www.ingramcontent.com/pod-product-compliance
Lightning Source LLC
Chambersburg PA
CBHW070917130626
46555CB00001B/175